OPERATION HANDSOME

MARGARET RYAN

Hodder
Children's
Books

A division of Hodder Headline Limited

To Jillian,
with love and thanks for all her help.

Text copyright © 2003 Margaret Ryan
Illustrations copyright © 2003 Nicola Slater
First published in 2003 by Hodder Children's Books

The rights of Margaret Ryan and Nicola Slater
to be identified as the Author and Illustrator of the work
respectively have been asserted by them in accordance
with the Copyright, Designs and Patents Act 1988.

10 9 8 7 6 5 4 3 2

A Catalogue record for this book is available
from the British Library

ISBN 0 340 87778 2

Typeset in ITC NewBaskerville by Avon DataSet Ltd,
Bidford-on-Avon, Warwickshire

Printed and bound in Great Britain by
Bookmarque Ltd, Croydon, Surrey

The paper and board used in this paperback by
Hodder Children's Books are natural recyclable products
made from wood grown in sustainable forests.
The manufacturing processes conform to the
environmental regulations of the country of origin.

Hodder Children's Books
a division of Hodder Headline Limited
338 Euston Road
London NW1 3BH

It was the start of another ordinary evening's homework: English, Maths, History. Why do teachers pile it on so much? Don't they know there's telly to be watched, computer games to be played, CDs to be listened to? I sighed and sorted the homework out into three piles on my desk.

Pile one. Homework I didn't mind doing: English: This was easy.

Pile two. Homework I didn't mind doing very much: History: English with dates.

Pile three. Homework I hated doing: Maths. No matter what the question was I always managed to get a six-figure answer.

I tackled the easiest pile first. Mrs Jackson, my English teacher, is always getting these crazy ideas for homework. Last week we had to imagine we were aliens landing on the planet Earth.

'Try to imagine you are seeing the planet for the first time,' she said. 'Write about your first impressions.'

I wrote, ... 'My first impression of the planet Earth is that it is owned by someone called McDonald. He keeps the inhabitants happy by feeding them hamburgers and slurpy drinks...' But I don't think that's what she wanted. She wittered on about mountains and trees and fast-flowing rivers. Sometimes I think *she's* from another planet, and I'm pretty sure she thinks the same about me.

This week the assignment was more personal.

'Write a short sentence or two about why you like or dislike something. Make it as interesting as you can,' she said.

OK.

LIKES

Velvet Guha, my best friend. I like her because she's a nice person and very organized, not like me at all. I think she could be Prime Minister one day, or, at least, Leader of the Really Sensible Party.

Andy Gray, my boyfriend. I like him because he's funny and doesn't talk about football all the time, like some boys. He's also got a mad Jack Russell terrier called Jack.

My mum, Eva Montgomery. I like her because she's my mum, although she is a lawyer, and a bit of a bossy boots at times.

My grandma, Aphrodite Harris, who's come to live with us recently from Australia. I like her because she's the sanest mad person I know, and she always does what she thinks is right, no matter what.

Sausage, egg and chips. I like them because they're yummy, especially if the egg is runny enough to dip my chips in. And not because it really annoys my mum, who's strictly vegetarian.

Words. I like them because . . . I just do. I like the look of them, the sound of them, the feel of them in my mouth. I like to learn new ones, especially big ones, and use them in conversation. Not just because I like to act grown-up. I just like words. OK? So I'm odd. So I'm weird. So what?

DISLIKES

Belinda Fisher (Fishcake). I dislike her because she never has a hair out of place and always looks like Little Miss Perfect, whereas I could win the Scruff of the Year Award, without even trying.

The Beelines – Belinda's no-brainer cronies. I dislike them because they do everything Belinda says and never think for themselves.

Wednesdays. I dislike them because we have double Maths on Wednesdays, and Mr Soames, my Maths teacher, says he is convinced I've had a numeracy bypass. Numeracy and bypass are my latest new words. I had to look them up to find out they were teacher-speak for rotten at Maths.

Lumpy custard and gooseberries. I dislike them because you should never ever have to chew liquid or eat anything hairy. Especially wearing a dental brace like mine.

Then I put down my pen. That was probably enough for Mrs Jackson to chew on.

I'm Abby, by the way. Abigail Montgomery. Star pupil at Cosgrove High. I made up the star bit. When I'm not in Stalag 3, our Siberian hut in the playground, I live at 3 Pelham Way with my mum, my grandma and our adopted dog, Benson. Benson used to belong to old Mrs Polanski along the road, but she got sick, so now he lives with us. Grandma organized that. She looks after Benson while I'm at school and Mum's at work. She looks after Mrs Polanski too; goes with her to the hospital and takes her shopping, etc. That's when she's not righting wrongs, organizing pensioner power, and generally pointing out to the world the error of its ways. I think she's great, especially when she gets me involved in some of her mad schemes.

This annoys my mum. Mum's very law-abiding. Very politically correct. Very Goody Two Shoes. Grandma's not. She wears real crocodile-skin boots, made for her by her second husband, Handsome Harris – the croc took on Handsome at wrestling and lost – and a smelly sheepskin jacket called Old Belle. Old Belle was Grandma's pet sheep when she lived on the sheep farm in Australia, and, when Old Belle went belly up, Handsome made her into a jacket for Grandma.

Handsome Harris isn't very PC either. He's on the run somewhere in Oz from the Australian mafia to whom he owes money. I'd love to meet him. He sounds great too. He's been writing to Grandma every week for months now, regular as clockwork. The letters usually arrive on a Tuesday morning, except, for the last few weeks, they haven't. That has upset Grandma. She pretended it didn't and laughed it off at first.

'Handsome's probably lost the address,' she said. 'He can be a bit forgetful at times.'

But then I could see her getting more and more worried, till this morning, when the letter didn't arrive again, and she slumped into herself looking really miserable.

I gave her a hug and tried to comfort her.

'Perhaps there's a postal strike in Oz, Grandma,' I said.

Grandma said nothing.

'Or perhaps the Australian government is on a tree-saving drive, and the shops have run out of writing paper.'

Grandma looked at me like I'd just come down from the trees.

'Or perhaps . . .' I searched what Mrs Jackson calls my over-fertile imagination for another explanation. 'Perhaps . . . perhaps . . . why doesn't he just phone like normal people?'

'Handsome hates phones,' said Grandma. 'He was hit on the head by one as a child. It fell off the wall and knocked him out. He hasn't touched one since.'

'Oh,' I said, and wondered why this explanation,

coming from Grandma, didn't seem at all unlikely. 'Well perhaps . . .'

'Perhaps the Australian mafia have caught up with him,' said Grandma, 'and he's dinner for the dingoes.' And she looked so sad I gave her another big hug.

'Please don't worry, Grandma. We'll find out what's happened to Handsome. Remember when you decided Mum needed a man to cheer her up, and we thought up "Operation Boyfriend"?'

Grandma smiled. 'That worked out really well.'

'Well, we'll do the same thing and call it "Operation Handsome". We'll think of something. Just wait and see. An idea will come along any minute.'

But, despite racking my brains all day, nothing had come to me – apart from a telling-off in History for not paying attention.

So, here I was, doing my homework, and no further forward. I wrote AUSTRALIAN MAFIA in big letters in my Dislikes column, then scored it out again. If I wrote a few sentences about *why* I disliked them, Mrs Jackson would only mutter again about my over-fertile imagination.

2

School wasn't too bad today, for a Wednesday. Mrs Jackson collected in the Likes and Dislikes homework, and handed out our next assignment – to read and comment on a newspaper article that had caught our eye. Some of the boys giggled, so she fixed them with her evil eye – the left one I think it was – and told them that that did not include comments on the naked ladies in the tabloids. The boys looked quite disappointed.

Some people muttered that they didn't get a daily newspaper, so Velvet said they could come into her parents' little post office, and she'd give them any spares left over from her paper round. That's why Velvet's my best friend, she's just so nice. Unlike Belinda Fishcake, who was already telling Mrs Jackson about an article she'd been reading about star signs: Aries, Scorpio, etc. Apparently Belinda's sign foretold that she was going to be beautiful and rich and famous. Naturally.

Belinda's a plonker. Star signs? What a load of old

nonsense! Who would believe anything like that? It's totally crazy to think that the pattern of little lights in the sky can affect your life . . .

Hmm. I wonder what the article said about *my* star sign.

Note to self: Read horoscope in daily paper – just out of interest . . .

I wish I hadn't bothered.

Apparently several planets were on a collision course, leading to a cosmic traffic jam. There was lots of trouble ahead for me, my horoscope announced gleefully, and I was advised to keep my head down, and not make any important decisions.

Load of old rubbish. I bet the tea boy makes up the horoscopes in his lunch break.

But then something else in the paper caught my eye: a report on a court case. I sometimes read those if Mum's been involved, though she wasn't this time. It said . . .

Malcolm McConnell (54) was sentenced to two years in Newton Open Prison at Avery Crown Court today for passing fraudulent cheques. Police said they had been after McConnell for some time.

Malcolm McConnell! I knew about him. So did Grandma. He was one of her old boyfriends from university. We had tried to find him some months before, when we were looking for a boyfriend for

Mum. We thought, or at least Grandma thought, that Malcolm might have a son that would do. I know it sounds a crazy idea, but Grandma has a way of making crazy ideas seem OK.

This one wasn't. We ran into the police at Malcolm's house and ended up at the police station for questioning. Mum wasn't best pleased about it. Mad as a snake actually. But it all turned out all right in the end. We did find Mum a boyfriend. He's called David Anderson and he IS the son of an old boyfriend of Grandma's. But now it looked like the police had finally caught up with Malcolm and he was in the nick.

I wonder what that's like. I wonder if it's the same as on the telly. I've only ever been in jail when I've played Monopoly. Then I thought WAIT A MINUTE. My over-fertile imagination went into overdrive. Malcolm McConnell was a crook. Right? Handsome Harris was being chased by crooks. Right? Perhaps Malcolm McConnell could find out for us what had happened to Handsome. Perhaps there was a sort of crooks' grapevine that could get us some information. I know it was a crazy idea. I was getting to be as bad as Grandma. But it was worth a try. I'd talk it over with Grandma and see what she thought. Of course, I'd have to wait till Mum was out of the way . . .

'Fancy a walk with Benson?' I said to Grandma after our bean casserole that night.

Grandma brightened up.

'Good idea, Abby,' she said. 'We could go down by

that new fry bar in the precinct and get ourselves some chips.'

Mum looked up from her law book, disapproval written all over her face.

'What is the point,' she said, 'of my trying to feed you two a healthy diet if you go and ruin it with chips?'

'Oh come on, Eva,' said Grandma. 'We go along with your faddy diet most of the time, but we've had so many beans this week, I can hardly move without far—'

'Don't use that word, please. You know I don't like it!'

Grandma grinned and picked up Benson's lead. Benson shot to his paws and raced us to the front door. He obviously fancied chips too. Grandma and I wrapped up warmly against the cold: Grandma in her crocodile boots and Old Belle; me in a baggy old sweater and scarf, and we headed out. Benson dodged on ahead of us doing his usual bloodhound impression. I waited till we had turned the corner at the bottom of the street before I launched into my idea.

'You know you're worried about Handsome Harris not writing any more, Grandma?' I said.

'Uhuh,' said Grandma.

'Well, you know your friend Malcolm McConnell? The one who's a crook,' I said.

'Uhuh,' said Grandma.

'Well,' I said, and handed her the report I'd cut out

of the paper. 'I thought we might go and visit him, and see if he has any crooked contacts in Oz who could give us some information about Handsome.'

Grandma put on her glasses and read the cutting by the light from the electricity showroom. They were offering a special deal on dishwashers. I thought I might mention that to Mum. Have *you* ever tried scraping burnt butter-beans off the side of a casserole dish?

Grandma sighed and handed me back the cutting.

'Poor old Malcolm,' she said. 'Still, he's probably better off in prison than in that horrible house he was living in. He'll be warmer and drier.'

'What about the visit then? Shall we go?'

'Your mum won't like it, Abby,' she said.

'I wasn't exactly going to tell Mum,' I confessed. 'Anyway we'd only be doing a good deed. Prison visiting.'

Grandma grinned. 'OK. I'll write to Malcolm and see if we can set up the visit.'

We carried on through the precinct to the fry bar. Benson was already sitting outside, dribbling expectantly. Now, it may have been my over-fertile imagination, but I could have sworn Grandma had more of a spring in her step. Probably the thought of doing something positive about Handsome. That and the prospect of a nice pile of greasy chips.

3

Mrs Jackson handed back our Likes and Dislikes homework today. Mine was mostly OK although the comment under what I'd written about Belinda was . . .

'She speaks highly of you too!'

I guess Belinda'd put me in her Dislikes column as well.

I don't know what it is about Belinda Fishcake, she just always seems to rub me up the wrong way. She's always so perfect. She must get up in the middle of the night to get herself ready for school. Her blonde hair's always shiny and freshly shampooed. It's dead straight too, like it's been ironed. She never has a bad hair day. I never have a good one. No amount of gunk discourages my hair from spiralling out of my head in a big bid for freedom. I never stand beside the garden fence for too long in case my hair attaches itself and I have to be cut loose with the shears. Belinda's teeth are straight too, unlike mine, which had to be put behind bars to keep them in check. Left to their own devices I'd need a duck's beak to cover them up.

Then there are the bosoms. Belinda's are bigger. Enough said.

As if that wasn't bad enough, she goes on about beauty all the time. What's in, what's out. She thinks she's some kind of a trendsetter. Honestly, if she was chocolate she'd eat herself. Except that she wouldn't, of course, because chocolate is fattening. Not that I have to worry about that. I could eat a mountain of chocolate and it would make no difference. I know because I tried it once and it only made me sick. I'm so thin, if I stand sideways, I disappear.

'You're slim, not thin,' said Velvet, when I moaned on to her about this at lunchtime. 'Think positively, Abby.'

'OK,' I said. 'I'm positive I'm thin.'

Velvet shook her head. 'Idiot,' she said, and gave me an onion bhaji from her lunch box.

Her lunch box is always much more interesting than mine. She has samosas and pakora and little ball things made with lentils. My sandwiches are always filled with either tuna or cheese.

I had just sunk my fangs into the cheddar when Belinda, followed by the Beelines, appeared in the dining room. The Beelines follow Belinda so closely you'd think they were attached by an umbilical cord. Umbilical's one of my latest words. I heard it in Social Education the other day. It's the cord that attaches you to your mum inside the womb, and finishes up as your belly button. In class we all ended up checking if we had an Inny or an Outy. Belly button, that is. We weren't supposed to be doing that. It's not part of the National Curriculum, as far as I know. We were just winding up Miss Frobisher because she's new and a bit dippy.

In case you're interested, there were more Innys than Outys, and, as a group, they were spectacularly unremarkable, except for one which sported a gold belly-button ring. Guess whose that was? Guess who said it was the latest fashion? Guess who showed it all round? Guess who gets right up my nose? Congratulations. You've guessed correctly. Belinda Fishcake.

And now here she was wrinkling her perfect little nose and sniffing. She always does that around Velvet because Velvet's mum gives her Indian food for lunch. The Beelines sniffed too. 'Aaargh! What a smell!' they said and walked on, holding their noses.

I jumped to my feet, scattering the contents of my lunch box.

Velvet grabbed my arm. 'Leave it, Abby,' she said quietly. 'There's nothing you can do.'

I picked up my grubby sandwiches. I knew there was nothing I could do, you can't stop people sniffing. But they made me so angry. There are more subtle ways of being racist than calling people names, and Belinda and the Beelines were experts at it.

4

I had a surprise at the close of school that day.
Grandma Aphrodite and Benson were waiting for
me at the school gate.

'We thought we'd walk you home today,' said
Grandma, 'just in case you were missing Andy.'

I grinned and blushed a little bit. I *was* missing
Andy. He's a good friend as well as my boyfriend.
Belinda Fishcake's never forgiven him for taking me
to the last school disco instead of her. But Andy was
away for a week on a school trip to an outdoor
adventure centre. He'd been phoning me every night
to tell me what he'd been up to that day. So far he's
been orienteering – good fun map-reading and haring
around the countryside; canoeing – great fun turning
canoes upside down and getting wet; and abseiling –
brilliant fun swinging on ropes down cliff faces. But
scary! Don't look down! Andy's in the year above me,
so I'll get a chance to do it all next year.

'The other reason we met you,' Grandma went on,
'is to discuss the evening meal.'

I looked at her. 'It's Thursday,' I said. 'It's always veggie burgers on a Thursday.'

'Ah, but only if your mum's cooking,' said Grandma, 'and tonight she's not. Tonight we have a reprieve. David Anderson phoned her at the office today to say he's got two tickets for the theatre, so the pair of them are eating out.'

'Aha,' I said.

Mum's romance with David Anderson was progressing nicely. He's the son of Grandma's old friend, Charlie Anderson, Professor of English at the university. David is a wonderful cartoonist with a wicked sense of humour. I like him. He makes Mum laugh a lot and she's nearly forgiven Grandma and me for organizing her meeting with him, accidentally on purpose.

'What shall we have to eat then?' Grandma grinned at me.

I grinned back. We both knew it would be our all-time favourite: sausage, egg and chips.

We walked home with Benson, stopping only to collect some sausages from Mr Ness, our local butcher. We also collected a bone for Benson. I waited outside the shop with Benson while Grandma bought the sausages. Benson pressed his nose up against the window and looked forlorn. Then he let out such a mournful howl that Mr Ness immediately brought him out a bone. Benson wagged his tail and gave Mr Ness a paw. That dog should be on the stage.

By the time we reached home Mum was already changing to go out. She was in indecisive mode, judging by the amount of clothes strewn on the bed. And she calls *me* untidy!

'Help me look for my new black high heels, Abby,' she said, when I poked my nose round the bedroom door. 'I can't find them anywhere.'

I looked at the sea of shoes littering the floor and wasn't surprised.

Then I looked at Mum.

'Would that be the new high heels with the patent leather toes?' I asked.

'Uhuh,' said Mum.

'Patent leather toes and sling backs?'

'Uhuh.'

'Patent leather toes, sling backs, and little silver daisies on the buckles?'

'Yes yes,' said Mum. 'Have you seen them?'

'No,' I said. 'Not unless they're the ones you're wearing.'

Mum looked down at her feet and tutted. 'Why didn't you say so before? Now help me zip up this dress. I'm sure it's going to be too tight. I'm sure I've put on weight, though I hardly eat a thing. Does it wrinkle at the back? How do I look?'

'Fine,' I grinned. 'Your bum doesn't look big in it at all.'

Mum gasped and twisted round to look at her rear in the mirror.

'I'm joking. I'm joking,' I said. 'You look great.

A dash of lippy and a splash of *eau de man-eater* and David doesn't stand a chance.'

Mum laughed and applied the war paint. She scrubs up quite nicely, for a mum.

The doorbell rang, and, despite the killer heels, she was off like the favourite in a horse race.

Grandma and I waved bye bye. Benson contented himself with thumping his tail on the floor. He wasn't moving from his bone.

'Well,' I said to Grandma. 'What do you think?'

'I think we did well to get that pair together,' said Grandma. 'Let's celebrate with some extra ketchup on our chips.'

But I wasn't celebrating at midnight. I was lying awake, unable to sleep. Not from an over indulgence in tomato sauce, or a dicky tum from a dodgy sausage, but because of the noise that was coming from the sitting room. Wall to wall Showaddy waddy. 'Under the Moon of Love' thumping out big time!

I shrugged on my Pooh Bear dressing-gown, stuck my feet into my matching slippers and went downstairs. Mum and David were sitting very close together on the sofa, singing along and sorting through their favourite records.

I coughed politely, but they didn't hear me.

I coughed again, louder. Still no reaction.

I coughed loud enough for an ambulance to be called and an intensive-care bed prepared. Nothing.

What did I have to do? Expire in front of them?

I had a better idea. I pulled out the plug to the music centre.

'Whaaaaat . . .'

At least that got their attention.

'Do you know what time it is?' I said. 'Don't you two have work in the morning? I can't get to sleep for the noise. Neither can half the neighbourhood. Isn't it time you two were in bed?'

And I swept out of the room, congratulating myself on my dramatic exit.

Then I heard them giggling. Then I realized what I'd said.

Then I went to bed and blushed till I eventually fell asleep.

5

Grandma continued to search the post each morning for a letter from Handsome Harris. But none came. What did arrive, though, was a letter from Malcolm McConnell telling Grandma he'd be delighted if she'd visit him in prison.

'I'll go as soon as I can,' Grandma whispered to me when Mum was out of earshot. 'That way I'll feel at least I'm doing something.'

'You mean *we'll* go,' I whispered back. 'Operation Handsome was *my* idea, remember?'

'But your mum won't like it.'

'Then we won't tell her.'

'Won't tell me what?' said Mum, suddenly appearing in the hall.

Honestly, that woman could hear the grass grow!

'What we're planning for your Christmas present,' lied Grandma smoothly.

Mum looked at us suspiciously. 'Isn't it a bit early to be planning for Christmas?'

'Ah, but you don't know what we're planning,' said Grandma.

Neither did I, but that was a minor point.

'I always worry when you two start whispering,' said Mum. 'It usually spells trouble. Usually for me. Anyway I can't stand here chatting all day. I must go. Don't be late for school, Abby.'

As if!

As usual I had to run to catch the bus. Good thing I have long legs. Long and skinny like a new-born colt. I reckon, if I really put my mind to it, or my legs to it, I could be an athlete. A famous athlete. I can just see myself at the Olympics, standing up on the winner's platform, receiving my gold medal for coming first in the all new 'Bus Catching' event. I was mentally taking my bow and waving to the admiring crowd as I sat down on a seat.

Unfortunately, it was already occupied. A large lady gave a yell and pushed me off her knee. I fell on the floor and squashed her dog. The cairn terrier gave a yelp and tried to take a bite out of my leg. He ripped my new black tights. I could feel my knee poke through and my face turn scarlet as I sprawled on the floor of the bus. I was all arms and legs and one bare knee. I struggled to get up, and apologized profusely to the large lady. To her dog as well. I felt such a fool. I could win a gold medal for being an idiot too. Fishcake had seen it all, of course, and smirked and tutted. That didn't help.

During English that day she had some news that didn't help either.

'Next week,' she announced to everyone, whether they wanted to know or not, 'my mum is opening a new beauty salon in the High Street. The salon's called "In the Pink", and it's going to be fabulous. There's a special opening offer of ten per cent off absolutely everything for my friends during the first week. So hurry along.'

Then she handed out flyers to everyone, even the boys.

'Give it to your mum or your sister,' she said, and gave them the benefit of her perfect smile.

I had a look at the flyer. It was done on cutesy pink paper with spidery handwriting. You could have loads of things done to your body including a toe tidy pedicure, temporary nails, or an eyelash perm and tint.

'Who would want these things?' I wondered.

I noticed it didn't offer teeth straightening or zit zapping; my personal beauty routine. I made a paper aeroplane out of my flyer, and was about to launch it when Mrs Jackson glared at me and I had to put it in my pocket.

It fell out of my pocket later on that night when I was emptying out all the other rubbish; empty crisp packets, gum wrappers, etc. Mum picked it up.

'What's this?' she said.

And, before I could reply, she went on, 'Oh, I bet this has to do with the Christmas surprise you were talking about with Grandma. I hope I haven't spoiled it for you. I won't ask any more questions, but I think it's a great idea. I'll really look forward to my beauty treatment, whichever one you choose.'

Traitor! Whose side was she on? If she thought I was going into Fishcake's mum's shop she was very much mistaken . . . but then Grandma and I would need to think up some other surprise for Mum's Christmas, and she'd seemed really pleased with that one . . . oh help! I could feel my face settling into its glum expression. This had not been a good day.

It improved later that night though, when Andy phoned me. He told me more about his course at the outdoor adventure centre.

'We went sailing today,' he enthused, 'in GP 14s.'

'What does that mean?' I asked. The only GPs I knew were in the health centre.

'The GP stands for general purpose and the fourteen is the length of the boat. Fourteen feet.'

'Cool.'

'Only if you fall in the water,' laughed Andy, 'which I did, but I was wearing a life-jacket and Lindsay helped haul me back on board.'

'Lindsey?' I said, my heart sinking into my boots. 'Who's Lindsey? I don't think I know her.'

'She's a he,' said Andy. 'A new boy in my year who's just moved to the area.'

'Oh right,' I said, and breathed a quiet sigh of relief. Not that I was jealous or anything.

Then Andy went on to tell me how they'd sailed round three markers, set in a triangular course, several hundred metres apart, and how he was nearly bopped by the boom when it came crashing across as they changed tack. It sounded like good fun.

'What's been happening with you, Abby?' he asked.

'Oh nothing much,' I said, 'apart from being bitten by a cross cairn terrier and going to jail.'

There was a gasp from the other end of the phone. I told him about my day and swore him to secrecy about what Grandma and I were planning to do.

'You and your grandma,' said Andy. 'You're always up to something.'

Then he asked me if I missed him, and if I was looking forward to seeing him again soon.

And I said . . . well, never mind what I said. That's private!

I'll have to do something about Mum. She's acting like a lovesick teenager, and it's all my fault. Mine and Grandma's. If we hadn't thought she needed a man in her life, if we hadn't thought up Operation Boyfriend, if we hadn't introduced her to David Anderson, if we hadn't poked our noses into her affairs, we might be able to get into the bathroom occasionally.

Mum just used to go in there for a quick shower; now she spends half the night. She lights scented candles, sploshes in scented bubble bath, and slaps enough cream on her face to cover a sherry trifle. And, she's started reading soppy romances. I caught her at it one day, reading one inside her law book.

'I'm really surprised at you,' I said. 'You'll never get to be a partner in the firm if that's how you carry on.'

Help! I sounded exactly like she does when I try to skip my homework.

But she just smiled dreamily, put on one of her silly old love songs, and started singing it to

Benson. Benson loves Mum dearly, but this was more than a dog could bear. He gave her the same look he gives her when she mentions the word BATH, and slid under the sofa. But Mum didn't care, she picked up a cushion and sang to it instead.

Weird or what?

I mentioned this strange behaviour to Velvet and Andy – he's back now safe and sound from his adventures. He brought me a notebook, a pen and some toffees from the outdoor adventure centre's gift shop. I use the pen all the time, and the notebook's in my blazer pocket next to my heart. I tried one of the toffees, but it got caught up in my dental braces and nearly sealed my mouth shut for ever. Now that *would* have been a disaster, so I gave the rest of the toffees to Benson and swore him to secrecy. He gave me his paw and promised never to breathe a word to anyone.

Andy and Velvet gave me their considered opinions on Mum's behaviour.

'Bit odd,' said Andy.

'Bit strange,' said Velvet.

'But perhaps that's how old people act when they're in love,' said Andy. 'How about your parents, Velvet? Do they act like that?'

'Oh no,' said Velvet. 'Only the parrot sings in our house, and that's just when he joins in with an ad on the television. Anyway my mum and dad had an arranged marriage, and that's a little different.'

'How does that work?' I asked, intrigued – this is one of my favourite new words.

'Well,' said Velvet, taking a long drink of her lunchtime juice. 'When my nanima and nana, that's my gran and granddad, thought it was time my mum should be married, they told all their friends that they were looking for a suitable boy for her. It was important that he was a nice boy from a good family. All the friends asked around and several boys were produced for my mum to meet. Eventually she chose my dad.'

'As simple as that?' said Andy.

'I suppose so,' said Velvet.

'But what if you didn't like *any* of the boys,' I said. 'Supposing they all looked like Danny Plover in 3B. He's pond life. He's just come out of the swamp. He's still evolving!'

'Poor Danny,' said Velvet. 'I don't know. I suppose you'd just have to choose someone.'

'Or no one,' I said.

Velvet shook her head. 'It's not good in Indian culture for a woman to be alone. It's good to be in a family. Families are important.'

I nodded. I could agree with that. Mum and I had been on our own before Grandma came over from Oz to stay with us. My dad had left Mum when he found out she was pregnant with me. She divorced him and hasn't seen him since. Grandma'd never liked him anyway, so he's never talked about in our house. But I do wonder about him sometimes. I look in the mirror and I wonder what bits of me are like him. I wonder if he ever wonders about me. About *his* family. Then I stop wondering because it only makes me sad or cross or both.

'That's one of the things I really like about David Anderson coming round to see Mum,' I said. 'Sometimes he brings his son, Peter, and his dad, Charlie, and the house is filled with our two families. There's noise and talking and laughter, and cups of tea, and chocolate biscuits and . . .'

'And it looks like you'll just have to put up with your mum's weird behaviour then,' Andy and Velvet grinned.

They're probably right.

It was prison visiting time, and I had that hollow, jittery feeling in my tum. I always get that when I'm doing something I probably shouldn't.

'What's Malcolm McConnell like?' I asked Grandma, as we got on the bus for the short ride to Newton Prison.

'Last time I saw him he had lots of thick, black hair and a cheeky grin,' said Grandma. 'But I expect he'll have changed a bit. People do.'

We didn't tell Mum we were going to the prison, of course. She thought I was meeting Andy. I was, but not till later. I did feel a bit guilty about not telling her, but she would only have got herself in a tizz, so I told myself it was for her own good.

We got off the bus and headed for the prison. I'm not sure what I expected it to look like. A grim, grey building with lots of iron bars on the windows, perhaps. But Grandma explained that this was an open prison, and these prisoners were not dangerous, so things were a bit more relaxed.

We found Malcolm McConnell sweeping up the last of the autumn leaves in the grounds of a big old house. He threw down his broom when he saw Grandma.

'Aphrodite!' he cried. 'It's great to see you. You haven't changed a bit.'

Malcolm had. He still had the cheeky grin, but most of the thick, black hair had gone.

'You look well,' said Grandma, returning his hug.

Malcolm nodded his bald head. 'Food's not wonderful here, but better than anything I could cook, and I get plenty of fresh air and exercise. I'm on garden detail. Clearing up mostly, at this time of year.'

'This is my granddaughter, Abby,' Grandma introduced me.

Malcolm and I shook hands. I'd never shaken hands with a crook before. It didn't feel any different.

'Well, tell me what you've been up to, Aphrodite,' he said cheerfully. 'No need to ask about me. Everyone knows what I've been up to. It's been all over the papers. I got into debt. I tried to get out of debt. Illegally. Eventually I got caught and ended up here. End of story.'

Grandma smiled sympathetically. 'It's debt I've come to talk to you about. I have a problem and I need some help.'

And she told Malcolm all about Handsome Harris. About him getting behind with his taxes and borrowing money from the Australian mafia to pay them, then selling off their sheep farm to clear all the debts. But how the crooks wanted more and more money, which Handsome Harris didn't have and couldn't pay.

'So he went on the run,' said Malcolm, nodding. 'It figures.'

'But now I haven't heard from him in quite some time, and I'm really worried,' said Grandma. 'And I wondered . . . I wondered . . .'

'We wondered,' I chipped in, 'with your connections with the underworld, if you might be able to find out for us what was happening in the underworld. Down under, that is.'

'I see.' Malcolm ran a hand through his non-existent hair. 'Well, you'd better fill me in on all the details. Fancy a cup of tea?'

Over tea we told him how we'd nearly been arrested trying to visit him at his house some months ago when we were involved in looking for a man for Mum.

'We thought you might have a son,' Grandma added, as Malcolm looked alarmed.

Suddenly I thought about Velvet's grandparents looking for a suitable boy for their daughter, and, in some ways, what we had done didn't seem a lot different.

'I don't have any children,' Malcolm confessed. 'Never got round to settling down somehow. Never met the right woman to keep me on the straight and narrow. Still, now there's you two. You'll come and visit me again, won't you? I'll get word to my friend

Willie the Weasel about Handsome Harris. If there's anything to be found out, he's your man. Meantime,' and he lowered his voice, 'I could always get you a dud cheque to tide things over.'

Grandma hesitated.

'No thank you,' I said firmly. 'Handsome's in enough trouble already.'

'Abby's right,' said Grandma. 'But thanks for the offer. You're a good sort, Malcolm.'

Malcolm's cheeks turned as pink as his head and he took a large gulp of his tea to hide his embarrassment.

Then the visit was over and Malcolm walked us to the front gate.

'See you soon,' he said, and was gone. He didn't wait to see us go through the gate. It must have felt strange that we could go through and he couldn't.

'He's a nice man, Grandma,' I said.

'He always was, Abby,' sighed Grandma. 'Nice, but weak.'

We got back on to the bus. Grandma stayed on and went to visit Mrs Polanski. I hopped off and met Andy at the café in the precinct.

'Well,' he said. 'I see they let you out again. How was prison? Dangerous? Scary? Exciting?'

I thought for a moment.

'A little bit sad,' I said.

8

Fishcake was insufferable today. I can't stand her. She came into school wearing pink socks, pink hair-slides and a pink badge on her lapel. It read: You too could be 'In the Pink' and beautiful. Ask me how.

All the Beelines had pink badges too. Naturally.

Belinda was holding court in the playground at morning break.

'I'm the retail beauty advisor for the salon on a Saturday and after school,' she told anyone within earshot.

Note that 'retail beauty advisor' bit. Not helping out in Mum's shop, or selling the face cream, like most people would say. But she hadn't finished.

'Come in and see me and I'll advise you on all the beauty treatments. How do you like my nails?'

I curled my ragged, chewed ones into my palms and stole a quick look. Belinda's were bright pink and sparkly; like she'd dipped them in Christmas glitter.

'Ooh, aren't they lovely,' cooed the Beelines.

'And my toes are matching,' Belinda preened.

'Super,' breathed the Beelines. 'We must get ours done! When shall we come in, Belinda? What about Saturday lunchtime?'

Belinda was drumming up plenty of business for her mum, and she'd get more from my mum too. That reminded me that Christmas wasn't that far away, and my piggy-bank was practically empty. I didn't think Grandma's would be much better. How were we going to afford the beauty treatments Mum thought she was getting for Christmas? They were quite expensive.

I talked it over with Andy at lunchtime while we stuffed our faces with salt and vinegar crisps.

'I was thinking about Christmas too,' crunched Andy. 'Perhaps we'll have to save some of our pocket money. Not spend it all on a Saturday, like we usually do.'

'What shall we do then? Stay at home? I don't fancy that much. Mum will insist I help with the Saturday shopping.'

'Perhaps we could do something to earn some Christmas money,' said Andy. 'What about car washing? My dad's always complaining about having to wash his.'

'That could be fun if we do it together,' I said.

'It wouldn't be any fun at all doing it without you, Abby,' he said, and grinned.

I grinned back and it was settled. I told Grandma our plans when I got home. Mum wasn't in so it was safe to talk. Then I showed Grandma the list of beauty treatments. She whistled as she looked at them.

'Strewth,' she said. 'Look at the price of a mud pack! We could collect some mud from the garden and charge a lot less than that.'

'You didn't have much of a beauty routine on the sheep farm then, Grandma,' I grinned.

'I did too,' she said. 'I washed my face and cleaned my teeth. Sometimes I even combed my hair. Not that the sheep were bothered mind, especially Old Belle. She loved me anyway. So did . . . does Handsome.' She pulled herself together. 'Well, looks like I'll have to earn some money for Christmas too.'

'Doing what?' Grandma's jobs never lasted long.

'Dunno,' said Grandma. 'But I'll think of something.'

She picked up Benson's lead. 'Come on, old fellow. Walkies.'

Benson raced her to the door and won.

An hour later they bounced back home.

'I've got it,' said Grandma. 'I've thought of something that will earn me some money.'

'What?' I asked.

'Guess.'

I pretended to think.

'Being a supermodel?'

'I'm too chunky,' said Grandma. 'But I might just be the right size for a Santa suit.'

'You're not going to wear a beard and be Father Christmas in the town centre!' I said aghast. 'Mum would never forgive you. Ho ho ho.'

Grandma threw a cushion at me. 'I thought about it,' she said, 'and went to ask. But I was too late. All the jobs had gone. They said, though, they usually only employed men. I don't see why. Who's to know who's behind that big beard? I shall take that up with them next Christmas.'

'What *are* you going to do then?'

'Dog walking. People are especially busy at this time of year and I'm sure there are some that would be happy to pay to have their dog walked regularly. I walk Benson anyway so . . .'

'Good idea,' I said. 'When will you start?'

'Right away. I've already put a card in the newsagent's window.'

Trust Grandma to waste no time.

The response to Grandma's ad was immediate. It's amazing the number of people who have pets they can't look after properly. Before long Grandma had a long list of clients, and Benson had a whole army of new friends. Some dogs were friendlier than others, a bit like people, I suppose, but most of them were delighted to be going out for long walks.

Grandma was really pleased.

'If this carries on,' she said, 'I may have to expand my business and take on a partner.'

'Who?' I asked, wishing I wasn't at school all day. Somehow I couldn't see Mum thinking dog walking would be a good career for me. She was always going on about homework and exams.

'Some of the pensioners are very fit,' said Grandma. 'I could ask Miss Flack.'

Miss Flack was a retired seamstress who had made me a really cool outfit for the last school disco.

'Miss Flack likes animals,' added Grandma, 'and the extra money would be useful to her.'

'I could help you after school some days,' I said, 'but not on a Saturday because I shall be busy with AACB enterprises then.'

'Alcoholics Anonymous – Children's Branch?' grinned Grandma.

'Abby and Andy's Cleaning Business. We're going into car washing.' And I gave her one of our little cards that Andy had done on the computer. Then I took it back. We only had one each.

'I wouldn't mind some help today,' said Grandma, clipping on Benson's lead. 'Some of the bigger dogs are a bit frisky.'

'OK,' I said. I was only going to start my homework and that could wait. A girl needs fresh air and exercise. Any excuse!

We collected our first dog in the next street. He was a mongrel called Mitch, and we found him tied up on a long lead in the garden. He was half collie, half Alsatian, and half daft. He nearly wagged his tail off when he saw us.

Not far away lived Pinky and Perky, bad-tempered twin Pekinese. They belonged to an old lady who couldn't get out much any more. The dogs were obviously spoiled and were so fat they waddled. They didn't want to go walkies, preferring instead their matching twin cushions in front of the television. But their owner insisted. The vet had warned her about their weight.

Two cul-de-sacs later we picked up Stalin. He was a Great Dane, nearly as big as me, but gentle with it.

Benson rushed up to him excitedly. These two were obviously pals.

One more stop to pick up Katy, a black Lab whose owner had just had a new baby, and we headed for the common. I had Benson and Stalin, and Grandma had the other four. I made it to the common first as Pinky and Perky kept stopping, wanting to be carried. Grandma would have none of it. She herded them along, probably like she'd done with the sheep on the farm in Oz.

The common was quiet as day faded into dusk, and mums with pushchairs headed home to make their children's tea. We let the dogs off the leads. Benson, Stalin, Mitch and Katy immediately began to play chases. Pinky and Perky sat down. Grandma threw a stick for them. They gave her a disdainful 'You threw it, you go get it' look, and she had to fetch it herself. I tried to coax them to play with a ball. No chance. They lay down side by side and went to sleep. These were serious couch potato Pekes.

After a while Grandma called Benson back. He came running and the other dogs followed on.

'Good boy, Benson,' I said, clipping on his lead. 'Good boy, Stalin. Good boy ... wait a minute, Grandma. How many dogs have you got?'

'Four,' said Grandma. 'Pinky and Perky. Mitch and Katy. There are six altogether. You should have Benson and Stalin.'

'I do, but there's another one.' And, even with my

numeracy bypass, I knew that four and three added up to too many dogs.

The extra dog was sleek and black, like a fast car or a fine racehorse. His eyes showed very white in his dark head, and he looked at us, and wagged his tail expectantly. A lead trailed from his collar and when he moved he limped. He stood there, one paw off the ground, waiting for us to act.

'Well, where did you come from, old fellow?' I asked, and picked up his lead. A silver disc hung from his collar, but I couldn't make out the name in the darkness.

'His owner can't be far away,' said Grandma, and we searched round the area till it was too dark to see.

'Right,' said Grandma. 'We'll just have to take him home with us till we can locate his owner. We can't leave the poor thing wandering around in the dark. Especially with that sore paw. Come on everyone. Home time.'

We dropped off all the other dogs and went home with Benson and his new friend.

Mum was home early and not in the best of moods.

'You're surely not bringing another dog in here?' she said the moment she saw us. 'We've got quite enough to cope with as it is.'

'Calm down, Eva,' said Grandma. 'The poor dog's lost. I just need to see what the disc on his collar says and I'll phone his owner and take him round.'

Mum sniffed and headed for the kitchen.

Grandma searched for her glasses.

'I'll look, Grandma,' I said. 'My eyes are better than yours.'

I knelt down by our sleek, black new friend and examined his disc.

'His name's Saturn,' I said. 'Good name. His address will be on the other side.'

But it wasn't. It had been, but time had rubbed it away and it was now so faint it was impossible to read.

'Uh-oh,' I said to Grandma. 'Trouble ahead. We don't know who his owner is. We can't take him home. Mum won't be best pleased. We'd better keep our heads down.'

Then something went PING! in my brain.

What was it my star sign had said???

10

To say Mum wasn't best pleased about Saturn is an understatement. Like saying Shakespeare was quite good at writing plays or Van Gogh wasn't too bad at painting. She exploded like a rocket at New Year.

'How is it,' she yelled at Grandma, 'that whenever you do something it always ends up in disaster? You look up an old friend, you get arrested. The school bus is under threat, your protest stops the traffic in the High Street. Mrs Polanski gets ill, we get her dog permanently.'

Benson definitely looked a bit hurt at this point. How could Mum call him a disaster, when he always gave her his undying affection? He crawled under the coffee table out of the way.

'And now,' Mum hadn't finished with Grandma yet, 'you get some crazy idea for earning money, and we just end up with another mouth to feed.'

'I haven't fed the dog yet,' said Grandma, quite unperturbed – i.e. not in the least bothered by Mum's rant. 'But I will, once I've looked at his sore paw.

Don't get into such a state about nothing, Eva. It's just a poor lame dog, not the end of the world. What's the matter with you? Is it your hormones?'

That was the WRONG thing to say.

Mum turned bright red. 'NO, IT IS NOT MY HORMONES!' she yelled, and stormed upstairs, adding just before she banged her bedroom door, 'And you can make your own dinner. Have chips with everything. Clog up your arteries. See if I care!'

Oops.

Grandma knelt down to examine Saturn's paw. 'I think your Mum's a little upset,' she said.

Another understatement.

'You feed Benson, Abby,' she went on, 'while I make up a poultice for Saturn's paw.'

She went into the kitchen and started making up some awful concoction. It smelled terrible, worse than Mum's bean casserole, after it's been through Benson. Even Benson wrinkled his nose at the pong, and he's not that fussy. But Grandma smeared the mixture on to an old clean cloth and strapped it to Saturn's paw. He licked her hand. Somehow, despite the smell, he seemed to know Grandma was trying to help him.

Grandma stroked his head. 'It's an old snake-bite cure I learned from Handsome Harris,' she said. 'But it fixes almost anything.'

'What about giving it to Mum then?' I muttered, as the phone rang.

I picked it up just as Mum lifted the upstairs extension. I heard David Anderson's cheerful voice. Now I know I should have put the phone down immediately, but, what can I say, I didn't. I eavesdropped. That's a much nicer word than snooped, don't you think?

I eavesdropped. Just a little bit. Just long enough to hear that Mum hadn't been made a partner in her law firm like she'd been hoping. The decision had been that day.

Oh dear. I put the phone down gently. So that was the real reason for the outburst. Nothing to do with Grandma or poor old Saturn. Poor Mum. What a shame. She works so hard too.

Then something struck me. David Anderson obviously knew when the decision was to be made, but we didn't. Mum had told him, but not us.

I felt slightly miffed, then it dawned on me that if she'd told David something important like that, things between them must be getting quite serious. Aha. Watch this space!

11

We had Saturn with us for two days. Grandma asked around, but no one seemed to know who his owner was; so Grandma decided to keep him till his paw was better before taking him to the cat and dog home.

'It's just for a couple of days, Eva,' she promised. 'We can't let the poor dog go out into a cold, friendless world with that sore paw.' Grandma really knew how to lay it on.

Mum scowled, but Saturn stayed. He was no trouble, apart from the awful smell of the snake-bite cure. Grandma was just checking his paw the following Saturday morning when the doorbell rang. I was still slobbing around in my Pooh Bear dressing-gown and slippers and went to answer it.

A strange woman stood on the doorstep. At first, with her long, black dress and long, black hair, I thought she must have been left over from a Hallowe'en party somewhere. Her fingers were stiff with silver rings, and silver chains with little bells on tinkled round her neck. Black eye shadow and blood-red lipstick gave her a witchy look, though when I looked more closely, the wart on her cheek turned out to be a little black stick-on star.

'Er, can I help you?' I asked. I nearly said, 'Where have you parked your broomstick?' but Mum says it's always better to be polite.

'Oh, I do hope you can help me,' she trilled. Her high-pitched voice was excited and a little squeaky. Not crackly or cackly. Not at all what I'd expected.

'I'm Ms Tickle,' she went on. 'I think you may have my dog here.'

Saturn gave a bark of recognition.

'You mean . . .'

'Saturn,' she said. 'After the planet.'

Uh-oh, I thought. Another one from another planet. Who needs little green men?

'He's here,' I said. 'Come in.'

She floated into the sitting room and Saturn bounded forward and knocked her over. No mean feat; she was a big lady. Saturn also knocked over the coffee table and the geranium Mum was desperately trying to keep alive. He stood on Ms Tickle's black hair, which turned out not to be her own, and the wig stayed on the floor, while she struggled to get up. Not easy with a five-stone dog sitting on your lap. I noticed her real hair was very short and even more carroty than mine.

I was just trying to stop Benson eating her wig when Mum found us.

'What *is* going on?' she said. 'I'm sure there

46

must be some perfectly simple explanation for this commotion, and I shall be most interested to hear it. Right now would be a good time.'

Honestly, she can be such a lawyer sometimes. I know she likes to have a lie-in on a Saturday morning, but there's no need to be rude.

I introduced Mum to Ms Tickle.

'Ms Tickle?' Mum raised her courtroom eyebrows. 'Is that your real name?'

'It's my professional name,' said Ms Tickle, now elevated to the sofa. Saturn sat at her feet licking the black-painted toenails, clearly visible through her open sandals. It was November but she obviously didn't feel the cold. I pulled my Pooh Bear dressing-gown more tightly round me. I also have a Pooh Bear cover for my hot-water bottle, but I don't tell anyone that.

'And just what profession are you in?' asked Mum, managing to make it sound like it might be the slave trade or gunrunning or drug trafficking. Certainly something dubious and highly illegal.

Ms Tickle drew herself up to her full height. Not easy when you're sitting down.

'I'm a clairvoyant,' she announced.

'Oh, a fortune teller,' sniffed Mum.

'No, a clairvoyant,' insisted Ms Tickle. 'I have a gift. I "see" things. That's how I knew where Saturn was. I "saw" him in this house in this street.'

'I see.' Mum was plainly unconvinced. 'Well, I've no doubt you'll be glad to get him back.'

'Oh, yes! My mum took him for a little walk the other day. Just around the block because of his sore paw, but she stopped to talk to a friend and Saturn just slipped away from her. He's a terrible wanderer.'

'Well, he didn't wander very far,' said Grandma. 'Just on to the common where we found him.'

'I can't thank you enough for looking after him,' smiled Ms Tickle. 'And look – he's not limping any more! How did you manage to fix his paw? I've been trying for ages with no success.'

'Just an old snake-bite remedy,' said Grandma and I together, and laughed. Mum rolled her eyes.

'You must let me pay you for your trouble,' said Ms Tickle and dived into a big black bag and got out her big black purse. I wasn't surprised to see it was covered in silver stars.

'Wouldn't dream of it,' said Grandma. 'It was no trouble.'

'Then I'll give you a reading instead,' cried Ms Tickle, and rummaged in the big black bag again and got out some tarot cards. She placed them neatly on the coffee table.

'Oh, I don't think we'd want anything like that,' said Mum. 'We're not into . . . that kind of thing.'

'Oh don't be such a stick-in-the-mud, Eva,' said Grandma. 'What harm can it do? I might learn something about Handsome Harris, and it's very kind of Ms Tickle to offer.'

'Yes,' I nodded enthusiastically, 'and it would give

me one over Belinda Fishcake. I bet she's never had a tarot reading.'

'Well, I'm having nothing to do with it,' sniffed Mum. 'I'm going to make some tea, and I'm using a tea bag so there won't be any loose tea leaves to be read!'

Ms Tickle nodded. 'I'm so sorry about your disappointment at work,' she called after her.

'What?' Mum wheeled round.

'But it'll come out all right in the end, you'll see,' said Ms Tickle. 'You just have to be patient.' And she began to turn over the cards.

Mum thumped into the kitchen and amid some quite unnecessary banging and crashing of kettle and mugs, Ms Tickle 'read' the cards for Grandma. She turned them over one by one and told us what she saw.

'There's a black cloud of worry hanging over you.'

Grandma nodded.

'But you must be strong. Don't let it overpower you. You also need to be more careful with money.'

'I know,' Grandma sighed. 'It just seems to disappear.'

After that there was some stuff about travel and a tall man coming into her life.

'That'll be Malcolm,' said Grandma.

But then Ms Tickle said something that did make me sit up and take notice.

'There seem to be a lot of strange men in your life,' she said. 'I see a lot of strange men.'

Oh no, I thought and hugged Benson. I bet the Australian mafia have contacted the UK mafia and they're coming to get us to pay Handsome Harris's debts. Then I thought of my piggy-bank. I somehow didn't think they would be willing to settle for a button and a hairy toffee. Perhaps they would turn up in a big black limo with tinted windows when Andy and I were doing our car washing. Perhaps they would leap out and demand money with menaces. Perhaps I should keep Benson with me for protection. I hugged him closer. Perhaps I should take Benson to school with me, in case the Australian mafia turned up there. But then what would Mrs Jackson say about my over-fertile imagination . . . ? Maybe she was right . . . Maybe I do let my imagination run away with me . . . Maybe.

'Abby, are you all right?' Grandma asked. 'You've gone a little pale.'

'Don't worry about the cards, Abby,' said Ms Tickle. 'They only give an indication of what might happen, and I interpret that.'

Really? I wasn't entirely convinced.

'You are a highly imaginative person, Abby,' went on Ms Tickle. 'Perhaps you may be a clairvoyant yourself in years to come.'

'I don't think so.' I tried to laugh things off. 'Not with a name like Abigail Montgomery.'

'You can always change your name,' said Ms Tickle. 'I did. My real name is Mavis Scruggs.'

Help, I thought. Mum had changed her name from

Godiva to Eva – well, wouldn't you? Grandma had changed her name from Agnes to Aphrodite – no, I wouldn't either. What would I change my name to? I found myself thinking about the possibilities. Hermione? Kylie? Madonna? Madonna Montgomery? Hmm. That did have a certain ring to it. Perhaps I was going to follow in the family tradition after all!

12

I couldn't wait to tell Andy about Ms Tickle alias Mavis Scruggs. He was coming round at eleven o'clock that morning to do the first car wash outside our house. Grandma had organized some of the pensioners to bring their cars round.

'Much cheaper than the real car wash,' Grandma had told them, 'and you don't have to sit inside the car and be menaced by those horrible big brushes.'

Major Knotts was first in the queue. He had forgotten to roll up his window last time he visited the car wash and had got himself washed as well.

'Memory,' he'd muttered. 'Not what it used to be.'

So he was delighted with our scheme.

'That's what I like to see in young people,' he said. 'Enterprise.' And he went into our house and had a cup of tea and a chat with Grandma while he waited.

Washing cars is much harder work than I thought, and wetter. I was soon thoroughly soaked, as was

Andy, but we were too hot to care. Rinsing off the soap suds I told Andy about Ms Tickle and her predictions. Andy was of the same opinion as Mum.

'Load of old rubbish,' he said.

That made me feel better, and I stopped looking over my shoulder for the approach of the Australian mafia. I was feeling quite cheerful till a large Merc came along the road and slid to a halt close by.

'Hullo,' said Andy. 'Looks like we're getting some more custom.'

But we weren't.

Out of the Merc stepped, not the Australian mafia with fat cigars and fatter beer bellies, but Belinda Fishcake. She was dressed entirely in pink, from the sparkly pink shadow on her eyelids to the tips of her dainty pink trainers. She looked like the fairy from the top of a Christmas tree.

But she didn't sound like one.

'So this is what you get up to on a Saturday,' she sneered. 'I thought you went out on a date, Abby.'

'We're just trying to earn some money for Christmas,' I said, trying to sound superior, which is difficult when your face is bright red and you're sopping wet.

'Oh, I am too,' smirked Belinda. 'Doing the beauty treatments in Mum's new shop. Did I tell you about it?'

'Several times,' I muttered.

'You should come along, Abby,' she smiled sweetly.

'I'm sure we could do *something* to help you. Though it would take some time, of course.'

And she jumped back into her dad's car so quickly that the wet sponge just missed her.

Pity.

13

I went home with Velvet after school today. Mrs Guha had invited me for tea. I couldn't wait. She's a great cook. Did I tell you I'm considering being a restaurant critic when I grow up? Imagine being able to eat in loads of fancy restaurants and get paid for it.

I mentioned that to Mum. She said she thought that restaurant critics were probably journalists as well, who'd most certainly worked very hard, and passed all their exams to get where they had. I was sorry I'd opened my big mouth. Mum manages to mention exams in just about every conversation we have. If I said the Slime Creatures from the Monster Swamp were coming to eat us, she'd probably say, 'Yes, well, pass your exams first and the Slime Creatures can eat you later.'

'Does your mum go on about exams?' I asked Velvet, as we walked home towards the little post office her mum and dad run.

'Yes,' said Velvet, 'but my dad's even worse. He

wants me to do well at school and go to university. He says a good education is a wonderful thing because no one can ever take it away from you.'

We went into the post office. It was long and narrow. Shelves filled with sweets, groceries and newspapers lined the walls. The post office counter was at the far end. Mrs Guha was behind it, helping an old lady fill out a TV licence form.

'Hullo, Abby,' she called. 'How are you? I shall be with you later. Go upstairs and eat something.'

Now that's what I like to hear. Velvet and I went upstairs to their flat and raided the kitchen. I had a kind of Indian pastry thing, both spicy and sweet at the same time. Yummy. Velvet had a Kit-Kat. Then we went back downstairs and I helped Velvet to fold the evening papers, ready for her round. We put them into two bags and, with me helping, popped them into the letter boxes in record time. After that it was home again for tea.

I love Velvet's flat with its wonderful aromas. Mrs Guha's kitchen is filled with large pots of herbs and jars with colourful spices. She chops up the herbs and grinds up the spices to put in her dishes. I helped her make the vegetable curry. I was fascinated by all the things that went into it: cumin, coriander, turmeric, chillis . . .

'You are a good girl, Abby,' she said. 'You will make a good cook one day. You like your food. Not like Velvet,' she sighed. 'That girl eats like a bird. A very small bird.'

'I eat like a bird too,' I said. 'A vulture.'

I helped stir the pots while Velvet set the table.

'Do you want a knife and fork,' she said, 'or will you use your fingers and some naan bread like us?'

'Fingers,' I grinned. 'Then I can lick them afterwards.'

'Have you spoken to Abby yet about Diwali?' asked her mum.

Velvet shook her head. 'I thought I'd wait till tonight. You can explain it much better than I can.'

'What's this?' I said. 'Isn't Diwali your Festival of Light?' I'd learned a little bit about it in primary school.

Mrs Guha nodded. 'It's our special time of the year.'

And she sat down and told me more about it.

'Diwali is held at the new moon in late October or early November each year,' she said. 'For Hindus, it marks the start of the financial or farming year, and for our community, the start of the New Year too. It commemorates the day when Lord Rama and his wife, Sita, returned home after fourteen years in exile. The lights of Diwali represent the candles that were lit to guide them safely home. We all get together with family and friends for a special celebration, and we wondered if you would like to come with us this year?'

'What do you think?' Velvet raised her eyebrows at me. 'Would you like to come?'

'Like to come? I'd love to come,' I said. 'What do I

have to do? Do I have to wear a sari? Do I have to learn to do Indian dancing? I can only do the disco stuff. Do I have to have a dot on my forehead? Do I have to . . .'

Velvet laughed. 'You don't have to "do" anything. Just come along and enjoy the celebration.'

I couldn't wait.

I couldn't wait for dinner to be ready either. It smelled so good. It was all vegetarian, but not like Mum cooks. Not a bean casserole in sight. I could be vegetarian all the time, if I lived with Velvet. I ate till I could hardly move. Mrs Guha was really pleased.

'See?' she kept saying to Velvet. 'See what a good eater Abby is. You should take a lesson from her.'

Velvet rolled her eyes. 'That's the last time you're coming for tea,' she said. 'You just get me into trouble.'

When we had finished eating. Velvet and I did some of our homework together, then we had a chat. We talked about school and boys. About families and boys. About music and boys. About boys and boys.

'I really really like Andy,' I told her for the umpteenth time.

'Really?' grinned Velvet. 'I'd never have guessed.'

'He's a nice person.'

'That's the best reason for liking him then.'

'What about you? Are there no boys you especially like?'

'I like lots of boys,' Velvet said, 'especially the funny ones. But just as friends. It's too early to be thinking of anything else. There are so many other things to do.'

'Like exams,' I sighed.

'And university,' said Velvet. 'And seeing the world and having adventures and becoming world famous.'

Actually, that didn't sound too bad. I wouldn't mind trekking in the jungle, so long as there was somebody else there to chase away the snakes. Or heading off to the Antarctic to chat to the king penguins, so long as I could take my Pooh Bear hot-water bottle. And being world famous really appealed. I could just see myself being introduced on TV as the world famous Abigail Montgomery. But famous for what? There really wasn't anything I was much good at. But I suppose I could learn to be good at something. Uh-oh, here we go, back to working hard and passing exams again. I pushed the thought away. Too much to contemplate on a full stomach.

'But *after* all that,' I said to Velvet. 'After you're Professor Velvet Guha, world famous scientist and explorer, will you have a boyfriend?'

'I might,' said Velvet.

'And an arranged marriage like your mum and dad?'

'Don't know,' said Velvet. 'Mum and Dad would probably like that.'

'Would you?'

'Don't know.'

'But you might.'

'I might.'

'If you do, can I come to the wedding?'
Velvet threw a cushion at me.
'You ask too many questions,' she said.
I could be world famous for that!

14

Isn't it funny how one thing can spark off another? After my conversation with Velvet about boys and marriage and the future, etc, I felt very grown-up. So, when I got home, I had another conversation with Mum. Grandma was pottering about up in the loft, so Mum and I were in the sitting room on our own.

'Did you have a nice time at Velvet's?' she asked.

'Yes,' I nodded. 'Velvet and I did some homework then we talked about boys and getting married.'

'What?' squeaked Mum.

'But we've decided to wait till we've passed our exams, been to university and become world famous for something or other.'

'That's all right then,' smiled Mum.

Then somehow that grown-up feeling made me open my mouth before my brain had a chance to catch up.

'But you didn't wait, Mum, did you?' I said. 'You were young when you married my dad.'

Mum coloured.

'Yes,' she said quietly, 'and I regretted it.'

Perhaps I should have left it there because Mum doesn't like to talk about my dad. I knew he left when he discovered Mum was having me because he felt he couldn't cope with the responsibility. Grandma had told me. But I was still curious.

'You never tell me anything about him,' I said.

Mum looked at me for a moment.

'What do you want to know?' she said.

'Everything. How you met him. Why you liked him. Why Grandma and Granddad didn't. Why you married him anyway. Why you don't like to talk about him. Why . . . oh, just everything.'

Oh, I was being so grown-up. Just like one of these smart-mouthed, know-it-all kids in the movies.

'You ask a lot of questions,' said Mum.

Now where had I heard that before?

'Wait here.'

Mum disappeared up into the loft. I could hear her shuffling about, moving things. I thought she'd just gone up to speak to Grandma, but a few moments later she was back carrying a plain brown box. On it there was a dusty white label with a name in Mum's writing. Martin Montgomery, it said. My dad.

'I knew you'd come asking questions one day, Abby,' said Mum. 'And you've a right to know. So, a long time ago, I put a collection of things into this box that might answer some of them. When you're ready, open the box and look through the contents.

When you've done that, I'll answer all your questions, if I can.'

Mum handed me the box. I gulped. This was more than I had bargained for. I didn't know what to say, so I just nodded and took the box up to my room. I placed it on my bed and looked at it for a long time. I'd always wanted to know more about my dad, but hadn't wanted to upset Mum by asking. Now, I'd taken the plunge, and here, perhaps, were some of the answers. I ran a finger over the clear Sellotape that sealed the box and felt the edge where the tape had been torn off. I picked at it. A little corner came up. I pulled at it gently. It started to loosen. Then I panicked and smoothed it back down. I wasn't ready yet. It had happened too quickly. I needed some more time to think. I wasn't as quite grown-up as I'd thought.

It was the night of the new moon and I was going to Velvet's house for Diwali. Velvet said her mum had been busy cleaning and polishing everything for weeks, and that she and her dad sometimes escaped to the cinema out of the way. Her mum had also bought them new clothes for Diwali. Apparently Lakshmi, the goddess of prosperity, would not visit scruffy people in a dirty house. I'd been fascinated by this and had told Grandma all about it.

'It's not so different from the old Scottish custom,' she said, 'of turning the house upside down and cleaning everything to greet the New Year. I remember my mother-in-law used to make sure even the rubbish bin was emptied just before midnight on New Year's Eve. Everyone dressed in their best clothes, shook hands and drank a glass of whisky as the town hall clock rang out the old year and rang in the new.'

'Whisky. Yuck!' I said.

'The children had ginger wine,' laughed Grandma.

'Your great granny Montgomery made her own. "Drink up. It'll keep out the cold", she always said. But it would have kept away the plague as well, it was eye-watering stuff.'

'Of course,' I said. I'd forgotten that Grandma's first husband, my granddad, was Scottish.

Mum dropped me off at Velvet's house and, when I looked up, I could see the candle burning in the window to help Lord Rama and Sita on their way. When I got to the door I looked for the Shathia, the symbol of good luck and prosperity, that Velvet told me would be drawn on the doorstep. And there it was, just beside the door mat.

Velvet had heard Mum's car arrive – she really would need to do something about that rattle – and was waiting for me. She looked lovely in her brand-new flame-coloured sari with the gold trim.

'You look fantastic,' I said.

'So do you.'

I'd worn my best trousers and blouse and had tamed some of my hair back with a scrunchie. I hoped Lakshmi would think I looked smart enough. I didn't want to let the Guhas down. After some Coke and crisps Velvet and I and her mum and dad went to the local community centre. It was brightly lit and full of people laughing and talking and laying food out on long tables. Mrs Guha went to place the food she had brought beside the rest. Velvet introduced me to lots of people.

'This is Auntie Jayshree. This is cousin Bidisha.

This is Dr Maini.' She seemed to know everyone.

'Come,' they all said. 'You must eat. Try this dish. Try that.'

I didn't need to be told twice.

Then the music started. A tall thin man, in narrow white trousers and a long tunic top, sat cross-legged on the floor, and began to play an instrument shaped like a big wooden box.

'It's a harmonium,' whispered Velvet.

He played traditional Indian tunes. They sounded strange to me, but nice. Some ladies started to dance. They were so graceful and their saris so colourful, I felt quite drab in my black trousers.

'Aren't you going to dance?' I asked Velvet.

'Not yet,' groaned Velvet, 'that comes later. All the mothers want to show how clever their children are and we all have to "do" something. We all have to perform. I hate it.'

Funnily enough Grandma had told me the same thing happened at Scottish New Year parties. My granddad, when he was a little boy, always had to sing. When it came to his turn he used to hide in the loo till he thought everyone had forgotten about him. They never had though, and when he finally came out he still had to sing all the verses of 'Scotland the Brave'.

'He hated that song for years afterwards,' laughed Grandma.

I had a great time at the Diwali celebration and clapped the loudest when Velvet performed her dance for everyone. I had my camera with me and took pictures of her. She was very good, but glad when it was over. She's really shy, unlike me. That's why I get so mad when Belinda and the Beelines are rotten to her.

Then suddenly an idea popped into my head. I know Velvet says there's nothing you can do about Belinda and the Beelines being nasty to her. That you can't accuse people of being racist just because they sniff and wrinkle their noses at you. But Grandma always says to me that when you know something's wrong, doing nothing's not an option.

So ... I did something. Nothing heroic, you understand. I'm not as brave as Grandma. I just wrote a story about going to the Diwali celebrations. I wrote about the food and the people and the colour and the light. Much as I've told you. I illustrated it with my photos and took it into school to show to Mrs Jackson.

She was delighted. Someone had actually written something without being asked! Plenty of Brownie points for me there, then! But, best of all, as I was certain she would, Mrs Jackson talked about my story in class. She talked about how important it was to understand and respect each other's cultures, and to enjoy the fact that we are not all the same. She pinned my story up on the wall and everyone, except you know who, crowded round and exclaimed over the food and the dancers, and Velvet's sari, and how lovely she looked.

I don't know if it did any good or not, but it made me feel better, and Velvet blushed to the tips of her ears, she was so pleased.

Belinda and the Beelines were not pleased. They made faces and turned their backs. Mrs Jackson wasn't pleased when she saw their reaction. She said nothing, but her look said it all.

Now that she has an idea of what's going on, I'm sure she'll keep a sharp lookout for Velvet.

Mrs Jackson may have beamed down from another planet, but basically she's OK.

16

Grandma got a letter from Malcolm McConnell today. She told me about it while Mum was soaking in the bath, singing at the top of her voice to one of her old tapes. She and David were going to an art exhibition that night, and she was really looking forward to it. She'd mellowed a little bit lately. Mellowed is one of my new words. Here it means Mum wasn't being quite so much of a pain as normal, though she still had her moments. Especially about homework. What is it about parents and homework? You'd think the earth would stop spinning if there wasn't enough homework done each night. That it only kept turning because children learned where the Rocky Mountains were, or about that square on the hypotenuse thingy. Just because I haven't copied out my French vocabulary doesn't mean *la fin du monde*, does it?

Anyway, Mum had improved a bit and it was all down to David Anderson. He and Mum were getting really, really friendly. Just about every sentence she utters these days is about how David says this or David does that. I hadn't really thought about Mum and David being serious about each other till now. How do I feel about that? Do I want someone else around permanently? Do I want to have to share Mum with David and his son, Peter? Don't quite know. I'll have to think about that. But things were serious enough for Mum to have invited David, Peter, and David's dad, Charlie, round to dinner this coming Saturday.

This was very unusual. We don't normally have people for dinner – we normally have vegetables. Rotten joke. Sorry! For one thing Mum's usually too busy with work and for another she can't cook. Nothing edible anyway. Nothing you would look forward to eating. I'm used to it, and Grandma says fortunately she has a cast-iron stomach and can eat anything, which is just as well.

To be fair, Mum is a very ethical person – she does what she thinks is right. A bit like Grandma, only in different ways. Mum's vegetarian because she doesn't think it's right to eat animals – though she just can't resist sweet and sour chicken sometimes – but what she does to the vegetables we have to eat isn't right either: so we have lots of prepared food from the chill counter in the supermarket, and Grandma and I sneak out to the chippie when things get too bad. But Mum, in a moment of madness, had invited David and his family for dinner.

'I don't know what I was thinking of,' she'd said to me before she disappeared into the bathroom to sing her heart out to Duran Duran. 'I've never cooked for lots of people before. What on earth will I make? Promise me you'll help, Abby. And, if you have any ideas . . .'

'We could always emigrate before Saturday,' I said, though I knew that wasn't really a helpful suggestion.

While Mum was soaking, Grandma told me about the contents of Malcolm's letter. She took it out of her jeans' pocket and smoothed it out.

'It's a bit cryptic,' she said.

'Uh-huh,' I said. I'd need to look that word up.

'It's not very clear what Malcolm means. I suppose it's because the letters are read by the prison staff before they're posted.'

'Aha,' I nodded knowingly. I was sure I'd seen that in a movie.

Grandma read the letter out.

Dear Aphrodite,
It was so good to see you and your lovely granddaughter the other week. You're so alike. I spoke to my friend about your little problem and he promised to look into it. He says he should have some news by the end of the week. Could you visit on Saturday for further details?
Your old friend,
Malcolm.

Grandma looked at me. 'Looks like I'm going back to jail on Saturday,' she said.

'I can't come with you this time, Grandma. It's Mum's dinner party and I've promised to help.'

71

Grandma nodded.

'Only thing is, Abby, can you walk the dogs too? I don't want to let my clients down and the dogs need their exercise.'

'No problem,' I said. 'I'll help Mum, then I'll take out the dogs.'

'Great,' said Grandma. 'I can't wait to find out what Willie the Weasel has discovered.'

Then the phone rang. It was Andy.

'Good news, Abby,' he said. 'My mum mentioned our car-washing enterprise in the staff room and the other teachers were very impressed. They're all bringing their cars round on Saturday. Looks like we're going to be really really busy.'

'Really?' I said. 'You don't know the half of it.' And for a moment I really did think about emigrating.

Then Andy and I had a chat about families. I think his is more normal than mine. He didn't agree.

'I have an older sister who jumps on the scales twenty-five times a day and lives on lettuce leaves, and a kid brother who goes to bed wearing a flying helmet and goggles, and you think that's normal?'

'But your mum and dad are normal,' I protested.

'No, they're not,' said Andy. 'My mum's a teacher and you *know* they're not normal. And my dad goes off fishing every weekend and catches old shoes.'

'At least you *have* a dad,' I said. 'He didn't go off before you were born because he didn't want the responsibility of a family.'

'True,' said Andy, 'but have you ever eaten old shoes for tea?'

'Sole and chips?' I said. 'Lots of times.'

'Anyway,' Andy went on, 'what's wrong with having a family that's interesting? Your mum's really clever, even if she is a pain sometimes, and your grandma's amazing. Look at all the mad things she does. And you're like her. You're pretty amazing too, I think. That's why I like you.'

'I like you too,' I said, and blushed so pink I could have got a job in Belinda's mum's shop.

I came off the phone still glowing. I really do like Andy. Did I mention that already?

17

The good thing about having good friends is that they're always there when you need them.

In school next day, I told Velvet all I had to do the following Saturday.

'How am I going to manage it?' I said. 'How am I going to wash cars, walk dogs, and help Mum cook, all at the same time? Now I'm getting into a panic.'

Velvet shook her head.

'Take one thing at a time, Abby,' she said. 'First of all the cooking. Your mum doesn't like to cook, does she? My mum does. Tell me what you want and my mum will do the cooking for you. She will make lots of dishes so you can help yourselves to what you want. You will have a splendid meal and your mum won't have to worry.'

'Would your mum do that?' I asked. Velvet made it sound so simple.

'Of course. Mum and I will bring the food round to your house in the afternoon then we'll collect Benson and the other dogs and take them for their walk. The post office closes early on a Saturday, so there is no problem.'

I gave Velvet a hug. 'Thank you for helping out.'

'Any time,' said Velvet.

Did I tell you my theory about time? I told my Science teacher and he said, 'Interesting, but not terribly scientific.' Which is teacher-speak for, 'this girl is a nut case.' See what *you* think.

Abigail Montgomery's Theory of Time.
Time speeds up or slows down depending upon what's happening in your life.

For instance, double Maths on a Wednesday can seem like an eternity. I look at my watch all the time and the hands never seem to move. In fact, I become convinced my watch has stopped. I give it a shake and check with my friends. Their watches say the same as mine. Odd, all the watches have stopped. I reckon there must be a strange magnetic field hovering over us, affecting all the watches. I suspect the approach of aliens. I look out of the classroom window to check. No aliens, unless they're invisible. Only a stray cat chasing an empty crisp packet. I look at the angle of the sun and wish I could tell the time by it. If the sun is at right angles to the town hall clock does that mean it's two forty-five and ten seconds precisely?

Then I remember my mobile phone. Mum only bought me it for use in emergencies. But knowing the time in double Maths *is* an emergency. Supposing it really *is* home time and the janitor has forgotten to ring the bell. Supposing he's fallen asleep, or has tripped and cracked his head on the old leaky boiler. Or the aliens who have been hiding behind the ancient pipes in the boiler room have got him! It's usually at this point, when I've just sneaked my phone out of my pocket, that Mr Soames says, 'Abigail Montgomery, do you *know* what time it is? Get on with your work!'

Whereas . . . If you're desperately waiting for your birthday to arrive, to get your sticky hands on a new CD player, time doesn't just stand still, it goes backwards. Or, if you're out on a Saturday afternoon with your boyfriend . . . time doesn't just fly, it disappears completely.

That's my theory anyway. Scientific or not.

The week of the dinner party, time went differently for Mum and Grandma. For Mum, with so much to do, there weren't enough hours in the day. She cleaned the house till it shone. She does this every once in a while, fortunately not too often, since she enlists the help of anyone standing nearby: i.e. me. She hauled out the dining-room table, usually covered in law books, and polished it. The dishes and cutlery normally only used at Christmas time were brought out and washed.

Benson watched all this activity anxiously. Benson's not keen on washing. He likes things smelly, especially himself, so when Mum had finally finished washing and polishing everything else in sight, there was only Benson left. He did his best to hide, but under the sofa in the sitting room just wasn't good enough – Mum found him easily. The tail he left sticking out was a big clue. Mum cornered him, picked him up, and put him in the bath. She slapped on the doggy shampoo and rubbed hard. Benson was affronted. Disgust was written all over him. If looks could have killed, Mum would have been in serious trouble. He stood there, trying to look doggily dignified, as he turned from butch Benson into peachy pup.

Mum took the shower rose down, rinsed him off and dried him with an old beach towel. And, as if that wasn't bad enough, the final indignity was the fluffing up of his coat with the hair dryer. He looked like he'd come out of Fishcake's mum's beauty salon. He hated it. He rolled around on the carpet, and did his best to get his scruffy old self back. But, try as he might, he still looked fluffy and smelled peachy. He was one unhappy dog.

Grandma was unhappy too. The days dragged by too slowly for her. She walked her dogs as usual, and, when she came home, tried to keep out of range of the spray polish Mum was scooting everywhere. But I could see she was distracted. Her mind was elsewhere. Saturday couldn't come quickly enough for her, whereas Mum needed at least two more Wednesdays and three more Fridays before then.

18

Saturday arrived the day after Friday. Mum was still in a panic, despite having gone round to see Mrs Guha about the food. I went with her to make sure she ordered my favourite chicken tikka masala, and samosas and pakoras and those round tasty things that look like big crisps. I was looking forward to this dinner party now.

Mrs Guha was delighted to help.

'I just love cooking,' she said.

'I don't,' said Mum.

Mrs Guha shook her head in disbelief. 'You will have to learn if you get a man. You will have to learn if you want to keep a man. Men need to be well fed. It keeps them happy and contented and out of trouble.'

Velvet rolled her eyes at me, and Mum opened her mouth to make a sharp retort, then remembered that Mrs Guha was doing her a favour, and shut it again.

'I'll make plenty of chicken and vegetarian dishes,' promised Mrs Guha. 'No one will go hungry. Then later,' and she beamed at Mum, 'when the dinner party has been a great success, I will teach you how to cook. You are an intelligent woman, you should be able to learn eventually.'

'Thank you,' smiled Mum, thinly, and we left before Mrs Guha could put her foot in it any further.

We got into the car and drove home. Mum was silent for a few moments.

'Cooking can't be that difficult,' she decided. 'Surely if you can read a recipe you can cook it.'

I said nothing. I knew Mum could read, but judging by her bean casseroles, she must be reading the cook books upside down in Finnish. Probably with her eyes shut.

Mum didn't have her usual Saturday lie-in. She was up while it was still dark, hoovering. The noise wakened up Grandma and she wandered downstairs, bleary-eyed.

'Are we expecting royalty or something? I'd have worn my best jammies if I'd known Her Maj was coming. Hoover that carpet any more, Eva, and you'll be through to the floor boards. Why are you in such a panic, girl? It's *you* David's coming to see, not how clean the carpet is.'

Mum ignored her and vacuumed a stray dog hair off the sofa. Benson thought about climbing back up again when she'd finished, but one look from Mum and he slid under the table instead. That didn't do either.

'Come out of there, Benson,' Mum ordered.

Benson squirmed back out and Mum had a severe word with him.

'Now,' she said. 'I want you to be on your best behaviour tonight. No sneaking under the table to look for crumbs. No sticking your wet nose in people's laps. No giving a paw and begging for food, and definitely no—'

'Farting,' said Grandma.

'Mum!' yelled Mum.

'Sorry,' grinned Grandma. 'I forgot you don't like that word.' So she had a word with Benson too.

'Now, listen up, young canine,' she said. 'At the merest hint of any flatulence – i.e. wind in the old gut bucket – kindly go out into the garden and point your bum at the moon. Got it?'

Benson wagged his tail. I choked on my cornflakes. Mum put her head in her hands.

As soon as Grandma was dressed Mum handed her a list of things she still needed from the shops.

'Sorry, Eva,' said Grandma. 'I can't manage to do that today. I'm too busy.'

'Surely you can spare half an hour from your dog walking?' Mum was miffed.

'Erm, I'm not doing dog walking today. Velvet and her mum are doing it for me when they come over with the food.'

'Velvet and her mum?' frowned Mum. 'So where are you going?'

'I have an appointment,' stalled Grandma.

'With whom?' asked Mum.

'An old friend.'

'Who is?'

I looked from one to the other. It was like watching tennis at Wimbledon. Right now it was advantage Mum.

Grandma hesitated. 'Malcolm McConnell.'

'Malcolm McConnell? Not the Malcolm McConnell you nearly got arrested going to see last time?'

'Uh-huh.'

'Don't you ever learn? Do you want to end up in the police station again?'

'That won't happen.'

'Why not?'

'Malcolm's already in prison.'

Mum sank down on to the sofa. The cushions she'd just plumped up sagged with her.

'Are you telling me you're visiting this man in prison?'

'Yes.'

'Is that wise? Prisons are not very nice places.'

'This one's an open prison. It's not too bad. Is it, Abby?'

Oops. Big mistake. I could see Grandma biting her tongue. But perhaps Mum wouldn't notice the slip.

Of course, she did. She's a lawyer, isn't she?

'Is it, Abby?' she said in a voice like cracked ice. 'Is it, ABBY?'

She turned to me. 'Have you been to this prison with your grandmother?'

Grandmother. Oh dear.

I looked at Grandma. She smiled apologetically and shrugged.

'Only once,' I said. 'But I'm not going today. I'm staying home to help you. Now what was it you wanted polished first? Andy and I are not starting our car wash till ten o'clock so there's plenty of time. Mrs Wilkinson's first. She's one of the teachers in Andy's mum's school. She has an old Mini, apparently. It's white with a black roof and you know how difficult white is to keep clean so . . .'

'Abby!' yelled Mum.

'You yelled?' I said, innocently.

'I want to know what you and your grandmother' – that word again – 'are up to.'

I looked at Grandma. She looked back at me. There was no way out of it. Mum would have to be told.

So we told her. At least we thought we did. We *thought* we told her that we were worried about Handsome Harris and were doing our best to find out what had happened to him. But, according to Mum, what we were really doing was . . . *consorting* – I love that word – with known criminals . . . getting ourselves *involved* with the underworld and putting ourselves in UNTOLD DANGER!!!

It sounded scary and exciting, but we told Mum it wasn't really.

'And we didn't consort,' protested Grandma. 'We only had a chat to Malcolm and then a cup of tea with him and his friends.'

'A crooked clergyman and a dodgy dentist,' I added helpfully.

'And Malcolm's going to contact the underworld,' said Grandma.

'Via Willie the Weasel,' I said.

'So we're not in any danger,' said Grandma.

'And we didn't accept the dud cheque.'

I probably shouldn't have added that last bit, but confessing kind of gets to you. I'd have been a hopeless spy. Tickle my feet and I'd tell you everything. Anyway Mum would have winkled the information out of me. I don't know why they don't make her a partner in the firm, she really is an ace lawyer. Then it dawned on me that maybe Grandma and I, with our little antics, weren't helping.

In the tirade that followed Mum mentioned this too, at great length. Grandma surprised her by agreeing.

'But I have to do what I can to find out what's happened to Handsome,' she said.

'You could always go to the police. That's what law-abiding citizens do,' said Mum tartly.

Grandma shook her head. 'Handsome wouldn't like that. He doesn't hold with policemen. Or any kind of authority really.'

'Now why doesn't that surprise me?' said Mum.

Grandma shrugged and got ready to go to the prison. I collected my bucket and mop. What a start to a Saturday.

19

I worked hard for the rest of that day. To get back into Mum's good books I collected the shopping she needed, set the table and arranged the flowers. Then I started work on the cars with Andy. Andy had found a hose in our garden shed and that made rinsing the cars a lot easier. Benson stayed indoors and watched us from the safe distance of the sitting-room window. There was no way he was getting anywhere near water again for some considerable time. Velvet and her mum arrived in the middle of the afternoon. They drove up in her mum's old, bent Astra and unloaded the food. There were lots and lots of dishes. It all smelled so delicious I was practically drooling. We put it in the kitchen, well out of reach of Benson, who was dribbling too, great big wet drips all over the floor.

Mrs Guha looked round the house.

'This is very clean and tidy,' she said to Mum. 'Very sparkling.'

'Thank you,' beamed Mum.

'Men don't like too much sparkling. Men like to be comfortable. Men like to lie around a bit. And scratch. Men like to scratch.'

Velvet collected Benson and took her mum away. Quickly.

I finished off the cars with Andy, and, when I came back into the house, Mum was just putting some candles on the table and sprinkling round some tiny silver stars left over from last Christmas. Then Grandma arrived home.

'Well,' I said. 'Did you find out anything?' I couldn't tell by her face.

'Yes and no,' said Grandma. 'Malcolm contacted Willie the Weasel, who contacted his pal Freddy the Forger, in Oz. He put out a few feelers, but so far, nothing. It looks like Handsome has dropped off the face of the earth.'

Or maybe son of crocodile boots has had his revenge, I thought.

Mum heard the conversation and put her arm round Grandma. 'No news is good news, Mum,' she said gently. 'You know what you always say. No worries, he'll be right.'

'Yes,' said Grandma. 'He'll be right.'

But she didn't sound convinced.

It was good that we had the dinner party that night to take Grandma's mind off things. Her old friend, Charlie Anderson, was just the one to cheer her up. He told stories of how things had been when he and Grandma had been at university together. About dressing up in crazy gear for Charities' Week, and jumping on and off buses, risking life and limb to collect money for good causes.

'Do you remember the Charities' Queen?' he asked Grandma. 'The stuck-up one, with her nose so high in the air she could hardly see her own feet?'

'Oh yes,' said Grandma. 'She came to the reception in the city hall, all dressed in pink, with a matching pink poodle. What a pain she was.'

Now who do you think that reminded me of?

I listened happily as I wolfed down Mrs Guha's tandoori chicken. I noticed Mum had a tiny taste too. Sometimes even the strongest weaken. Peter Anderson, David's son, tucked in as well.

'This is miles better than my dad's cooking,' he said. 'We usually get welded beans on toast. I wonder how they get the tandoori chicken that red colour. I don't suppose it's blood.'

'It's a paste they spread on,' I informed him. I'd seen Mrs Guha make it several times.

Grandma and Charlie, sitting beside us, tucked in like they'd never seen food before. Old people really can eat. Mum and David sat at the other end of the table and gazed at each other. When they weren't gazing, they were giggling. When they weren't giggling, they were giving each other little bits of food to taste; like they couldn't possibly try it for themselves. How soppy can you get? I heard Mum confess to David that she hadn't made the food herself, that she'd asked Mrs Guha to do it.

'But you thought of it, and you set the table so beautifully,' said David.

Mum nodded and smiled. I opened my mouth to protest, but thought better of it, and stuffed in another samosa instead. Mum was happy, Grandma had cheered up, and this food wasn't half bad. Only Benson was looking a bit miserable, lying in the corner with his head between his paws. I nudged Peter, nodded towards Benson and slid some food into my napkin. I excused myself from the table and when the adults weren't looking, sneaked the food to Benson. He gobbled it up. A few minutes later Peter sneaked him some too. Benson cheered up considerably. He loves Indian food. He always gets the left-overs from our takeaways.

But he had a slight problem with it which I'd forgotten about. He reminded us about it some time later when he experienced some wind in the old gut bucket, and completely forgot to go into the garden and point his bum at the moon!

Really, some dogs have no manners at all.

20

It was assembly time the following Monday. We have it in the hall of the main building of Cosgrove High. The main building is an old stone one covered with ivy. It looks really nice, but the janitor mutters that it's the ivy that's holding the building together. But, it's good to get out of Stalag 3 and feel part of the rest of the school.

The hall was filled with rows and rows of chairs. Mr Doig, the head teacher, waited patiently while we all filed in and sat down. After a bit, he thought we were settled, and was about to speak when someone coughed. Then someone else and someone else. Suddenly there was an epidemic. Everyone had to cough. It ran along the rows in ripples like a noisy Mexican wave.

Mr Doig was not amused.

'Dear dear,' he said. 'If the coughs are that bad, I'm sure a visit to Nurse McLennan will soon fix them.'

The coughing stopped abruptly. Nurse McLennan does not suffer fools gladly. She's a big lady, with a bosom big enough to keep books on. My mum knows her slightly and says she comes from Edinburgh.

Mr Doig said all the usual assembly things; about not running in the corridors, holding open doors and not dropping litter. It seemed there had been an extra problem recently with flyers for a new shop in town littering the school playground.

'Disgraceful,' I tutted quietly, but loud enough for Belinda, who was sitting in front of me, to hear. I'm sure her neck turned a brighter shade of pink.

Then Mr Doig launched into his 'Cosgrove High and its strong links with the community' speech. He went on about how we must be part of the community, take part in the community and be community-minded. I think community may be his favourite word. Everyone wondered where this was leading, then he got to the point. He wanted us to bring in Christmas gifts for pensioners. This was to be part of our community effort.

Aha, now we knew what he was on about. Bring in a gift for a pensioner. No problem. We discussed this on the way back across the playground to Stalag 3. Mrs Jackson tried to hurry us up, but it was a crisp, sunny morning and everyone took their time.

'I know what I'm going to bring in,' said Belinda. 'My mum has a new gift range of pink tissues. I'll bring in a box of those.'

'Good idea,' said the Beelines. 'Tissues are always acceptable to old people.'

I thought of the pensioners I knew. Mrs Polanski hated tissues.

'One good blow and they fall apart,' she said, 'and you're left with a handful of snot. 'Snot nice!'

Mrs Polanski always bought herself men's big white hankies in the January sales. Major Knotts still has boxes of army surplus hankies from when he had his shop, and Mr Hobbs, who was delighted to be in his second childhood, always made rabbits' ears out of his. Miss Flack embroidered her own. They were a work of art. It seemed a shame to blow your nose on them. A bit like eating your dinner off the Mona Lisa or hanging your anorak on Michelangelo's statue of David – I hope you're impressed by my artistic knowledge. I've really been listening while Mad Max rabbits on at Art.

No, I didn't think pink tissues were a good idea at all. The pensioners I knew would like something more original. Something less boring. But what? I would have to think about that.

'I think we've had enough delay for one morning,' said Mrs Jackson, when she had finally shepherded us back into Stalag 3. 'Now take out your poetry books and turn to page 6. Abby, will you read the first verse of "The Charge of the Light Brigade" for us, please.'

I groaned inwardly. Why did she always do this? Why did she always pick on me? She knew I had half the output of a small steel mill attached to my teeth, and if there were too many 's's in a word I sounded like steam escaping from a leaky pipe. Not only that but I'd been to see Mr Douglas, my dentist, the day before, and he'd examined the braces.

'Good good,' he said. 'Steady progress. Steady progress.' Then he proceeded to get out his little key and tighten them up.

'Aaaaargh.' I could feel the teeth move in my mouth. I could feel the roots loosen in their sockets. I could definitely feel them wobble.

'My teeth will all fall out now,' I told him, when he'd finally finished, and I found I could still talk.

'No, no,' he said. 'You'll be fine. You'll be fine.'

I'm sure he said everything twice to convince himself.

But I wasn't convinced as I read the poem. I didn't bother scanning it for 's's. The way I felt, if I opened my mouth too much, all my teeth would land on my poetry book, and I'd have one giant lissssp.

Being a teenager is not easy.

21

Grandma decided to take on Miss Flack as assistant dog walker. Miss Flack was delighted. She is really quite shy and didn't have many friends till Grandma took her under her wing. Now nearly everybody knows her.

I was lending a hand too, and we were out on the common one afternoon when we met Ms Tickle and Saturn. Saturn nearly pulled his owner off her feet as he bounded across to greet Grandma.

'Hullo, old fellow,' said Grandma. 'How's your paw?'

'It's fine,' said Ms Tickle, as Saturn was too busy licking Grandma's hand to reply.

'Ms Tickle, this is Miss Flack. Miss Flack, this is Ms Tickle.' I introduced the ladies to each other.

See – manners – Mum would be pleased!

'Hullo, Miss Flack,' beamed Ms Tickle.

'How do you do, Ms Tickle?' murmured Miss Flack.

I don't think she'd seen anything like Ms Tickle before.

'How's your arthritis?' asked Ms Tickle. 'It must be difficult for you to do your sewing sometimes when your hands are sore.'

'Oh,' I said, feeling a bit stupid. 'You two know each other already.'

'No, no,' laughed Ms Tickle. 'Just me "seeing" things.' And she looked at Grandma. 'I know things are worrying for you just now,' she said. 'But they'll work out all right. Keep yourself busy.'

And with that she called Saturn and they wandered off.

'Well, I never,' said Grandma. 'How does she do that?'

Miss Flack shook her head. 'How did she know about my arthritis and my sewing?'

I shook my head too. Crazy lady. Yet . . .

Grandma was quiet on the way home. She had on her thinking expression, so I chatted to Miss Flack. She was going to make me an outfit for the school Christmas disco. The last little 'designer' number she'd made for me had been a great success, and I'd worn it loads of times since then. The last time at Diwali.

'But please don't worry about making me anything if your fingers are painful,' I said. 'I can wear the same trousers and top again.'

'You certainly cannot, Abby,' she smiled. 'I have my reputation to think about.'

I grinned and Miss Flack grinned back. She really was a nice lady.

Grandma was still a bit quiet over dinner. We had broccoli and cheese bake. Is broccoli supposed to be brown and crunchy?

'Everything all right, Mum?' Mum asked.

'Mmm,' said Grandma.

That could have meant anything.

Then, over toffee yogurt pudding, Grandma finally said, 'Yes, I think it would work.'

'What?' asked Mum.

'Expanding my business,' said Grandma. 'I can't be a dog walker all my life, now can I? You would want your mother to have ambition, Eva, wouldn't you?'

Mum was cautious. Grandma was up to something.

'What exactly are you planning to do?'

'Well, I've been thinking,' said Grandma. That much we knew. 'I've got the dog-walking market more or less sewn up, with Miss Flack's help, so it's time to move on.'

'Where to?' asked Mum.

'To the garden shed,' said Grandma. 'If that's all right with you?'

'You want to move into the garden shed? Is this some kind of weird Ozzy winter migration thing? Did you used to go and sleep with the sheep when the nights were cold?'

'No no,' said Grandma. 'I'm not moving out there. I just want to use it for my business.'

'Which is?' said Mum.

'Curing sick animals. It just came to me this afternoon when I saw Saturn bounding around. I know lots of old cures. Handsome taught me them. I could use them to earn some money. Alternative medicine's very "in" just now.'

'And it would be "in" in our shed,' said Mum.

Grandma nodded.

'And not "in" in our house.'

'Oh no,' said Grandma.

'Well, so long as you keep all the potions and smells away from the house,' said Mum, 'I don't suppose it can do any harm.'

Famous last words!

22

One thing you can say about Grandma Aphrodite is that she never does anything by half. Early next morning we were wakened by some hammering and banging coming from the garden shed.

'What's that noise?' I asked Mum, as I groped my way downstairs. I don't really do mornings.

'Well, either Old Belle has come back from the dead, and is trying to communicate, or your grandma is up to something.'

Uh-oh, Mum was in sarky mode. She doesn't do mornings either.

'I'll just nip out and see,' I said. I was still half asleep, but curiosity is a powerful thing. I pulled my dressing-gown tighter round me, stuck my bare feet into my wellies – ooh chilly – and crunched out across the frosty back-garden grass. The shed door was open and a bit of old plank stuck out ready for me to trip over. I obliged. I hugged myself tight and breathed out cloudy air.

'Morning, Grandma,' I said. 'You're up early. Is this

another new job for you, early morning alarm calls for the entire neighbourhood?'

Grandma straightened up from her hammering. She was covered in dust and white paint.

'Couldn't sleep for thinking about my new business idea,' she said, 'so I just had to get up and get on with it. Do you remember that old plank we rescued from the skip when you were practising to be a model?'

I nodded. I'd tried to walk along it and pretend it was a catwalk. Perhaps a cat *could* have walked along it. I fell off.

'Well, I thought I'd use it as a sign for my new business and put it up on the side of the shed.'

I stepped into the shed and had a look. Grandma had cut the plank to size, sanded it down and attached a chain to it. Along the front she had painted in bold lettering, PETS' PROBLEMS.

'I'm going to hang it up on the side of the shed,' said Grandma, 'on those big nails I've just hammered in. You could give me a hand if you like.'

I lifted one end of the plank and with Grandma on the other we staggered and slipped across the frosty grass. Eventually we managed to hang the plank from the side of the shed.

'There,' beamed Grandma, 'how does that look?'

I looked at the enormous letters. Any moon men with problem pets would know where to bring them.

'It's not exactly subtle, is it, Grandma?' Subtle's one of

my favourite words at the moment. It can mean low-key or muted, but Grandma's sign was about as muted as a brass band practising in a tin hut.

'It pays to advertise,' said Grandma. 'Now how about some breakfast? I'm so hungry I could eat a horse sideways.'

She settled for two bowls of muesli and a toasted bagel while I hurriedly got ready for school. I said goodbye to Grandma and set off for a hard day in Stalag 3. I did my best to work hard, but it was difficult to concentrate on lessons as my mind kept drifting back to what Grandma was getting up to at home. That may have been why, when I dropped and broke an entire box of test tubes, Mr Burnett, the Science teacher, said I was about as much use as a chocolate teapot.

By the time I got back Grandma had fitted the shed out with the rickety table Mum usually uses for wallpapering, and an old white painted chest of drawers that used to be mine. It still had pink elephant stickers on the front. A camping gas stove and some battered pots and pans sat in the corner. It wasn't high tech, but then, neither is Grandma.

'All you need now are some customers,' I said.

'They're coming tomorrow,' beamed Grandma. 'I phoned Ms Tickle and she's bringing her friend, Thelma, who's been poorly.'

'Thelma?'

'A goat,' said Grandma. 'And I put a card in the newsagent's window and Mrs Polanski said she would announce my new business at the pensioners' club.'

'You're not curing pensioners too?' I grinned.

'Well, if my cures work on animals . . .' she said. 'Who knows. But I don't know how your mum will feel about this.' And she brought out a Pets' Problems sign she'd made for the front gate. Like the one on the side of the shed it wasn't exactly subtle and it had big black paw prints painted on it as well.

'I don't think I'll wait around while you show it to her,' I said.

'Perhaps I'll just hang it on the gate and hope she doesn't notice.'

I snorted.

'And there are these too,' said Grandma. 'I bought them this morning. They were going cheap in the joke shop.' She showed me some huge, luminous dinosaur footprints.

'They're made of some kind of resin, and you put them on the ground so that people can follow them round to the shed. What do you think?'

'I think when Mum sees all this you'd better stand well clear.'

In actual fact Mum wasn't too bad. She was in a really good mood when she came home because she'd met David for a drink after work. Introducing her to David was certainly one of Grandma's better ideas. Mum didn't think much of the Pets' Problems scheme, but said she was prepared to put up with it for a few months to see how it went. But, if it was a disaster, or if the neighbours complained about the signs, it would have to stop.

'No worries,' said Grandma.

Not yet, anyway.

23

The thing about Grandma Aphrodite is, everyone knows her. She realized, back in her teens, when she changed her name from Agnes to Aphrodite, that everyone would remember her. And they do. For a variety of reasons. It's not everyone you see walking down the street wearing a smelly old sheepskin jacket and crocodile boots, in charge of six dogs. So, word of her Pets' Problems business soon got round. And it was amazing the number of problems that there were. Thelma, the goat, who was now living in the back garden while Grandma monitored her condition – Grandma thought she might be depressed – was just the start. Next came a call from a Mr Smith. 'Is that Pets' Problems?' he asked Mum, who answered the phone.

'No, I mean, yes,' sighed Mum, who'd been hoping it was David.

'Well, my mynah bird seems a bit peaky and I'd like you to have a look at him. Can I bring him round in the morning?'

Mum checked with Grandma and ten-thirty was arranged. At ten-thirty prompt Mr Smith drove up in a little blue van. He got out carrying a mynah bird in a tall cage and followed the dinosaur footprints round to the shed.

'This is Mortimer,' he told Grandma. 'He's not been quite himself recently. I don't know what's wrong with him.'

Mortimer winked a beady eye at Grandma.

'He looks all right to me,' said Grandma. 'Bright eyes, glossy feathers. What have you been feeding him?'

'I'll show you the packet. It's in the van,' said Mr Smith. He went to fetch the food and never came back. Grandma waited and waited. Then she went out searching for him. She took the dogs and hunted everywhere. But there was no sign. She checked with Mum, but Mr Smith had left no address, and, with a name like Smith, there was no point in checking the phone book.

'Looks like we've been landed with a mynah bird,' said Grandma. 'A perfectly healthy mynah bird, as far as I can see.'

'But why would anyone want to do that?' said Mum. 'Why would anyone want to abandon a valuable bird?'

'Perhaps they were disappointed he doesn't talk,' I said. 'He hasn't said a word since he's been here.'

'Perhaps there's something wrong with him,' said Mum. 'Perhaps he's lost his tongue.'

Mortimer looked at Mum and winked a beady eye. 'Don't be so bloody stupid,' he said.

That was how we found out Mortimer could talk. That was how we found out he had a very full vocabulary. That he probably knew more words than Professor Anderson. It was just that most of the words were rude. I grinned when I heard him. Here were some more words for me to learn. Grandma laughed like a drain when she heard him. Mortimer's language was more colourful than some of the sheep hands' on the farm, she said. Mum was not amused.

In fact as Mortimer would have said, she was really 'bloody annoyed'.

24

I've discovered one of the differences between Mum and me. She likes a quiet peaceful life with everything neat and tidy. I don't. I like things happening. I like surprises. And, of course, I don't do neat and tidy.

That's one of the things about me that annoys Fishcake. She was holding a beauty forum in school today. A 'beauty forum', for goodness' sake. All it meant was she was surrounded by the Beelines as she expounded – my newest word, i.e. went on and on – about her mum's shop, and all the beauty products that are for sale. All the Beelines are frantically saving up their pocket money so they can go there before the Christmas disco and be beautified. I'm saving up too, of course, so that Mum can go there as her Christmas present. She was looking at the flyer again the other day and wondering about having the revitalizing facial. I looked at the price and gulped.

'I don't think you should bother,' I said. 'I'm sure David loves your wrinkles.'

Me and my big mouth. Forget about the career in diplomacy, then.

Mum flew to the mirror. 'What wrinkles?' she screeched.

'Er, I meant . . . smile lines.'

'What lines?' she yelled, and pulled her face this way and that.

'Um, I expect they're just natural creases.'

'CREASES!!!' Mum was beginning to sound like Mortimer.

He now lives in his cage on top of a little table in the sitting room. Grandma reported our acquisition to the police, but no one had been in looking for a lost mynah bird, and we couldn't get rid of him in case his owner came back. I'd begun thinking about that. Supposing Mr Smith had had sudden amnesia on his way out to his van and didn't know who or where he was. Or . . . supposing he was a bank robber and Mortimer was the only other person (OK, bird) left alive who knew where the loot was stashed, and had been left with us for safekeeping. Or . . . my fertile imagination was working overtime again, and I had just got to the bit where ghostly grey aliens were waiting for Mr Smith in the van to spirit him away when . . .

'Ugly mug, ugly mug.' Mortimer had obviously been following the conversation between Mum and me with interest.

'Shut up, Mortimer,' I said.

'Shut up, Mortimer,' said Mum.

'Shut up, Mortimer,' cackled Mortimer. 'Heh heh heh.'

So there was definitely no way out of the Christmas present. Mum's determined to get dewrinkled.

'Your mum was in the shop the other day,' smirked Fishcake, as I walked past, pointedly ignoring the beauty forum. 'She came in to get a full price list, so either she cares about how she looks or she's going to *try* to do something about you.'

The Beelines tittered.

'You can't improve on perfection,' I said loftily.

'You certainly are a perfect . . . scarecrow,' Belinda laughed. 'You should forget about the car washing and just go and stand in a field. I'm sure the farmers would pay you to scare away the birds.'

The Beelines laughed uproariously, like she'd said something really funny.

I walked away in dignified silence. At least I hoped that's how it looked. Actually I was a little bit hurt, and couldn't think of anything to say. Unlike me, I know. But I'd let Belinda get under my skin.

Later on I told Velvet what she'd said. 'I'm not really that scruffy, am I?'

Velvet gave me a thoughtful look. 'Pretty much,' she smiled. 'But that's how we like you. Don't worry about Belinda and the Beelines. Better to be a scruffy, nice person than a horrible, tidy one.'

My thoughts exactly.

But, when I went home that day, I may have taken the stains out of my school tie with a damp cloth. I may have pressed my school skirt with a warm iron, and I may have sewn the missing button back on my blazer, pricking my finger in the process and bleeding all over my school shirt. I thought about polishing my shoes as well, but I didn't. Enough was enough. I didn't want to risk turning into a horrible, tidy person.

Mum and I were on our own that evening as Grandma had gone to visit Mrs Polanski. Mrs Polanski had got a letter from the hospital with an appointment to get her bunions done, and Grandma had gone to see her to organize the transport. Mum was doing a crossword and I was doing some personal reading. *To Kill a Mockingbird*. Benson was doing nothing as usual and Mortimer was fast asleep.

Mum looked up. 'It's really quiet and peaceful this evening, isn't it? I like quiet and peaceful. Do you remember when we had a lot more quiet, peaceful evenings, Abby?'

I nodded. 'Before Grandma came.'

Mum sighed. 'Yes.'

'Before Benson.'

'Uh-huh.'

'Before Mortimer.'

'Yes. It was nice.'

'But before David too,' I said slyly.

'That's true,' Mum was thoughtful. 'Perhaps it's best not to have too much peace and quiet,' she said.

Uh-huh.

25

It was as well Mum got her evening of quiet and peaceful because life got a bit hectic after that.

For a start, Grandma's Pets' Problems business got busier and busier. Grandma definitely had a way with animals. They seemed to like and trust her, and were happy to come and see her. She chatted to them and sang to them. She even recited poetry. I found her in the shed one day telling a barn owl with an injured wing, that the owl and the pussycat went to sea in a beautiful pea-green boat. The owl put his head on one side and seemed reassured by the sound of her voice.

Thelma, the goat, was still with us and had been joined by Tinkletap. Grandma thought Thelma's depression might be helped if she had a friend, so now we had two goats cropping the back-garden grass. Mum didn't mind that, but they ate the washing as well. They'd had a good nibble at several pairs of her best knickers before she realized. There had been a minor volcanic eruption then, measuring about five out of ten on the Mother Scale.

Some wild ducks appeared in the garden too. No one knew where they came from, apart from the sky, that is. Grandma reckoned they just flew over and saw a friendly place to land. We had no duck pond, so the ducks – we named them Quackers and Cheese – would probably have flown on, if Grandma hadn't inflated my old paddling pool and filled it with water for them. The ducks seemed to like their blue and white striped pond and happily settled down. I got used to them quacking me awake in the morning, and the duck eggs were delicious. The back garden was completely taken over. The neat and tidy – i.e. boring – back garden had disappeared and chaos had taken its place. It was great. Fortunately, the neighbours liked the animals too, and were always coming round to see the latest addition, or to get some duck eggs for breakfast. Our back garden had never been so busy.

'Like the High Street at rush hour,' Mum muttered.

Or 'Aphrodite's Ark', as the neighbours said.

Grandma liked that.

Mum put up with it because it made Grandma happy. It made some money too and Grandma and I were well on our way to affording the beauty voucher for Mum's Christmas. Speaking of which, I'd had a brilliant idea for a present to take in to school for the pensioners' Christmas . . .

It started with my visit to Mrs Polanski. I'd gone with Grandma to see her and I told her about Mr Doig's pensioners' gift scheme.

'It's a nice idea,' said Mrs Polanski, 'but what will you buy?'

'Dunno,' I said. 'Everyone's talking about socks or soap or hankies, but I think that's boring.'

Mrs Polanski nodded her white head. 'Come with me, Abby,' she said.

She hobbled into her bedroom and opened the top drawer in her dressing table.

'Have a look,' she said.

I looked. Inside were lots of pairs of unused fluffy pink bed socks and enough bars of scented soap to wash an army of pensioners.

Mrs Polanski smiled at me. 'Why not use that famous imagination of yours and come up with something original. Something that will make a pensioner smile.'

So I thought and thought and came up with my brilliant idea. Andy and I went to buy the present after school. It didn't cost as much as I thought, so I bought one for Mrs Polanski too. I'll put it under her tree at Christmas time.

I told Mum and Grandma about it when I got home. Grandma laughed.

Mum said, 'You bought *what* for the pensioners?'

'Stick-on snake tattoos,' I said. 'Much more imaginative than socks or soap or hankies and just think of the fun they can have with them on Christmas morning. They can stick them on and pretend to their relatives they're real. They'll probably think Granny's gone bonkers. Probably think she'll be buying black leathers and a motorbike next, and hanging out with a gang of Hell's Angels, vrooming down to the post office on her mean machine to collect her pension.'

'Good thinking, Abby,' grinned Grandma.

'Good grief,' said Mum.

Then, as if Mum wasn't annoyed enough, Grandma dropped her bombshell.

'I had a letter from Malcolm today,' she said.

'Your crooked friend,' said Mum snippily.

'Uh-huh,' Grandma was unperturbed. Completely not bothered.

That's what I'm going to be next time Fishcake annoys me. Unperturbed.

'He hasn't got any more news about Handsome's whereabouts, but he's asked me to go and visit him. I've already written back to say it's not easy at the moment, with the dog walking and the Pets' Problems business being so busy.'

'Good,' said Mum.

'So I've invited him here next Saturday for tea instead.'

'You've WHAT?'

Now where have I heard that screech before?

'Invited him here,' continued Grandma. 'He's allowed out occasionally, you know. It's an open prison, and he's not dangerous, poor soul. He's got no family, so I didn't think you'd mind.'

'You don't think full stop,' yelled Mum. 'I'm a lawyer. I'm hoping to be made a partner in the firm.

You invite a convicted criminal for afternoon tea, and you didn't think I'd *mind*.'

'It's not against the law to be kind to criminals, is it?' asked Grandma. 'If it is, the law's an ass.'

For the next ten minutes Mum left Grandma in no doubt as to whom she thought was the ass. But, in the end, she calmed down and said she would be out shopping when Malcolm arrived, and she was sure he would be gone before she came back.

'OK,' said Grandma. 'I'll write him another letter telling him not to come to the front door wearing the ball and chain.'

I laughed, but Mum didn't think it was funny at all.

26

In the end, Grandma invited the pensioners round for tea as well. She did her dog walking early, and was just buttering her home-made scones, when they arrived. Andy and I had finished our car wash early too, so we lent a hand to butter/eat the scones.

'Is he here yet?' whispered Mrs Polanski, when I opened the front door to her. 'I've never met a real, live criminal before.'

'I've baked a cake, but it doesn't have a file in it,' giggled Miss Flack, when she arrived.

'I've brought my stick, just in case,' muttered Major Knotts. 'You can't be too careful with these johnnies.'

Mrs Hobbs had brought Mr Hobbs, who wouldn't leave home without his model aeroplane kit.

They had all just settled down when Malcolm arrived. He wore dark trousers and an anorak and looked very ordinary. Not scary at all. The pensioners seemed a bit disappointed. Then Malcolm began telling them tales of Willie the Weasel and Freddy the Forger, who was much smarter than Malcolm, and still on the 'outside'. But best of all he gave them some good advice about how to avoid being conned.

'Never buy anything at the door,' he said, 'and never ever let anyone into your house that you're not absolutely sure about. Even if they say they're from the gas board or the council or the police. Always ask for identification and phone and check it out.

'There are some terrible people out there,' he added, with a straight face.

The pensioners were delighted with him.

'Perhaps next time you're allowed out, you could come and speak at our pensioners' club,' said Mrs Polanski. 'You could give us the lowdown on the low life. It's good to have some inside knowledge about what crooks get up to. No offence.'

'None taken,' grinned Malcolm, and had another slice of Miss Flack's cake.

A stray crumb fell from his plate and eagle-eyed Benson caught it in midair with a snap of his jaws.

'Bloody good catch,' squawked Mortimer.

'Ooh, what a rude bird,' giggled Miss Flack.

'Give us a kiss,' chirped Mortimer.

Miss Flack blushed to the end of her nose.

Andy and I sat and listened to the chat and stuffed ourselves with more scones and cake.

'I love coming to your house,' said Andy. 'There's always something going on. Your grandma's amazing.' Then he whispered, 'And so are you.'

That just made my day. Belinda Fishcake, eat your heart out.

The pensioners and Malcolm had a great day too, though they'd all gone by the time Mum got home. But we were still talking about it.

'Did you see how Miss Flack just loved Mortimer?' I said. 'And he was so chatty to her.'

'And Major Knotts shook hands with Malcolm and wished him well,' said Andy.

'He's going to visit him in prison,' said Grandma, 'and everyone's going to send him Christmas cards. It's really good he's got some friends now.'

Mum said nothing, just bustled about putting the shopping away.

'Would anyone like some tea?' she asked brightly.

'No thanks,' we all said. 'We've had ours.' And we went on talking about our afternoon.

Mum looked a bit downcast. And I was sure, though she'd never admit it, that a little bit of her wished she'd had afternoon tea with Malcolm and the rest of us.

27

Just when Mum thought life had settled down, and Grandma couldn't get any more wild notions, Grandma decided to hold a séance. I know it's a mad idea, but she was just so worried about Handsome, she'd try anything.

It was Ms Tickle's idea really. She and Grandma had talked about it when Ms Tickle brought over Tinkletap to keep Thelma company. I was busy patting the goats at the time, and trying to stop them eating my jumper, so I was only half listening. Anyway, I sometimes think Ms Tickle's elevator doesn't go all the way to the top floor. Mad as a hatter, in fact.

Grandma was more polite. 'A bit other-worldly,' she said.

'Off her trolley,' said Mum.

But Ms Tickle was only trying to help.

'You've had no more word of Handsome Harris,' she said to Grandma, over a cup of tea in Grandma's shed. It was a statement, not a question.

'No,' said Grandma, 'not a thing. I'm very worried.'

'Hmm,' said Ms Tickle. 'There is something else we could try.'

'What?' said Grandma. 'I'll try anything.'

'We could hold a séance.'

'What?' yelped Grandma. 'You really think Handsome's dead? You really think he's gone to the big sheep shed in the sky?'

'No, no,' soothed Ms Tickle. 'I don't, but if we hold a séance we could ask my spirit guide. He's a Native American chief. You may have heard of him. Chief Sitting Bull.'

'He's your spirit guide?' Grandma was sceptical. 'I thought he was just in the old movies.'

Ms Tickle shook her head and her silver chains tinkled.

'He has been a great help to me, and if we can contact him he may be able to reassure you that Handsome is still alive.'

Grandma looked doubtful, then she made up her mind. 'What harm can it do?' she said.

I was so surprised I let go of the goats. Grandma's not the hocus-pocus type. What was she thinking about? What was *I* thinking about? Thelma and Tinkletap had just eaten a hole in my sleeve. Eaten a hole? Can you eat a hole? I would have to ask Mrs Jackson about that.

To be honest I didn't think Grandma would go through with it. I thought perhaps she just didn't want to hurt Ms Tickle's feelings. But no, the séance was on, and what's more, it was 'on' in our house. I assumed Grandma would have gone to Ms Tickle's house, but she had the decorators in, and said the smell of paint would get up Chief Sitting Bull's nose.

Apparently if conditions aren't absolutely perfect for him, he goes all huffy and won't communicate.

So, 3 Pelham Way was to be the site of the séance.

I told Andy and Velvet about it and swore them to secrecy.

Velvet giggled and moaned and pretended to go into a trance.

'Is there anybody there? One knock for yes, two knocks for no,' intoned Andy. 'It's a mad idea, Abby.'

'I know,' I said. 'I'm sure that's what Mum's going to say.'

'You mean she doesn't know?' said Velvet.

'She'll go bananas,' predicted Andy.

He was right.

'You're having a WHAT?' she said when Grandma finally told her.

'A séance,' said Grandma, looking a bit uncomfortable. 'Just a little one. We're not having a whole roomful of people or anything.'

'I should hope not,' said Mum. 'The fewer people who know you've finally flipped your lid the better.'

Flipped your lid? Very unlawyer-like speak.

Then Mum relented. 'Look, Mum,' she said. 'I know you're worried about Handsome, but this is crazy.'

'Perhaps,' said Grandma, 'but it can't do any harm.'

And it *was* just supposed to be a little séance, but Grandma told Mrs Polanski about it and she told the other pensioners, and they all asked if they could come. So did Velvet and Andy.

That's how we ended up with a whole roomful of people one Thursday after school.

Ms Tickle didn't mind.

'Chief Sitting Bull likes an audience,' she said. 'He's a bit of a drama queen. But you must be very quiet and still while I try to contact him.'

She sounded so matter of fact, like she was just going to phone the plumber or something. We all sat in our sitting room, not daring to move, while Ms Tickle lit two white feathers and wafted the smoke about.

'Just to make him feel at home,' she said.

She was wearing a multicoloured blanket over her black dress. She said that was for authenticity too, though I was sure I'd seen it for sale in the mill shop in the precinct.

When we were all very still, our eyes watering from the smoke, she began. She sat bolt upright in Mum's favourite chair and rolled her head till I thought it would drop off. Then she slumped forward and began to speak. We all craned forward to listen. Her high-pitched voice was very childlike.

'Chief Sitting Bull, Chief Sitting Bull, can you hear me? It's little Mavis.'

I thought the 'little' was pushing it. She was a lot of Mavis under that black dress.

'I have a question for you. Do you have Handsome Harris with you on the other side?'

We all listened. Nothing, except for a slight wheeze from Major Knotts' chest and a rumble from Andy's tum. I squeezed my lips together tightly to stop myself from giggling. Ms Tickle was deadly serious.

She had another go.

'Chief Sitting Bull, Chief Sitting Bull, can you hear me? Do you have Handsome Harris with you on the other side? One thump for yes. Two thumps for no.'

I could feel Andy's shoulders heave. He nudged me and I nearly burst out laughing. It was as well I didn't, for we all heard it, quite distinctly. Two thumps.

Everyone gasped. The silence was broken and Ms Tickle – alias little Mavis – came out of her trance.

Grandma beamed and everyone began talking at once. Then we opened the window to get rid of the smell of burnt feathers, and it was cups of tea all round.

Everyone congratulated Ms Tickle.

'Better than anything that's on afternoon telly,' said Mrs Polanski.

'Very interesting,' said Major Knotts.

'A little bit scary,' said Miss Flack.

'I'm sure it's a trick,' said Andy to me, 'but how did she do it?'

'Dunno,' I said. 'You were here, you saw what happened. And just look at Grandma, I haven't seen her so cheerful in ages.'

Later, when Mum came home and heard what had happened, she looked at Grandma's beaming face too.

'Well, if it helped,' she was all she said.

It was only later on, when I was playing with Benson, that I noticed the noise Benson's tail makes when he thumps it on the floor. It was very like the thumps that afternoon. Trouble was I couldn't remember whether Benson had been in the sitting room at the time or not. He has a habit of sneaking under the sofa for a snooze. But I kept my suspicions to myself. There was no point in upsetting Grandma. But Operation Handsome was becoming crazier by the minute.

And it didn't end there.

28

After a while Mum got used to the Pets' Problems business being in our shed, though she shuddered every time she passed the luminous dinosaur footprints on the grass. They certainly were a talking point. People stopped at the front gate and pointed. We were never going to win the Best Garden of the Year Award, or be in a glossy magazine, but they did help publicize Pets' Problems.

And don't people keep weird pets? We were downright boring with just a dog and a mynah bird. Over the space of a few days, Grandma treated a snake with halitosis-ssssss or bad breath-thththth, an albino crow with feather loss, and a constipated iguana. But, she did have to tell a small boy, who brought her a jar containing his lifeless stick insect, that what was in the jar was, in fact, a stick. He went off quite happily, vowing to ask his mum for a goldfish.

Then, one Sunday afternoon, when Mum was over at David's house, helping him hang new curtains, and

I was supposed to be doing my homework, Grandma and I spent some time pottering in the garden. We were chatting to the goats and feeding Quackers and Cheese, who had now been joined by two more ducks we called Bacon and Egg, when a customer appeared. He was a small, wiry man with straggly grey hair and a large tubby bulldog. The ducks scattered at their approach, but Grandma smiled. 'Hullo, can I help you?'

'It's Perce,' said the thin man, indicating the bulldog. 'He's usually such an old sweetie pie, but for some reason he's been a real grumpy box lately.'

Perce gave a menacing growl just to prove it.

'Now now, Perce,' said Grandma sternly. 'That's quite enough from you.'

Perce growled again, but more quietly. Grandma fixed him with a stare and growled back. I'd never heard Grandma growl before. Growling's not something you usually associate with grandmas. It was awesome. Perce thought so too. He subsided on to the ground with a loud sigh, and hung his big pink tongue out to steam in the cold afternoon air.

'How'd you do that?' asked the thin man, amazed. 'How'd you get him to behave? I took him to the vet last week, but Perce bit him and wrecked the surgery. I daren't go back.'

'Hmm,' Grandma hunkered down and held out her hand to Perce. He sniffed it cautiously then gave it a rasping lick.

Then Grandma sniffed and wrinkled her nose. 'Mr er . . . what did you say your name was?'

'Eassle. William Eassle.'

'Mr Eassle, are you wearing perfume?'

Mr Eassle looked affronted. Then his face cleared. 'Oh, it's not mine. It's Marlene's. New girlfriend,' he added coyly. 'She sprays it on like fly killer. Anyone standing within range gets it. Makes my eyes water sometimes.'

'And gets up your dog's nose, I think,' said Grandma. 'Dogs have very sensitive noses and the perfume, I'm sorry to say, smells like cats' pee. I don't think your dog likes cats.'

'You're right!' cried Mr Eassle. 'I knew I'd smelled that smell before.'

'Then I suggest you either buy Marlene some new perfume or get a new girlfriend,' smiled Grandma. 'That way I think you'll have your old sweetie pie Perce back again.'

'I don't think I'll bother with another girlfriend,' said Mr Eassle. 'They only upset Perce. Sometimes girlfriends are more trouble than they're worth. You know where you are with a dog. Thanks very much. Now how much do I owe you, Aphrodite?'

'How do you know my name?' asked Grandma.

Mr Eassle tugged at his collar and looked a bit shifty.

'Heard it about, like.'

'About where?'

'Oh, just around and about.'

I looked up from patting Perce who was now rolling over to have his tummy tickled. He really was an old sweetie pie. I scratched under his chin and noticed his disc. The name on it was W. W. Eassle.

Then something went PING in my brain.

'You're Willie the Weasel,' I cried.

Mr Eassle jumped like he'd been shot.

'How'd you know that?'

I pointed to the disc. 'I put W and W together with your surname,' I said. 'It's not rocket science.'

Willie the Weasel looked a bit shamefaced. 'Look,' he said. 'Don't tell Malcolm I came. He'd have a fit. He didn't tell me where you lived when he asked me to find out what I could about Handsome Harris. He just said his friend, Aphrodite, needed some help. But when I needed help with Perce, and heard about Pets' Problems, and how some people called this place Aphrodite's Ark, I just put two and two together. Aphrodite's not a name you forget, you see.'

'I see,' said Grandma.

'But don't you worry,' went on Willie the Weasel, 'you've helped Perce. I'll see you're all right. You're as safe as houses now from us criminals. You're one of us.'

'Thank you,' said Grandma, who could see he meant it sincerely.

Help, I thought. Friends in low places. We mustn't tell Mum.

Willie the Weasel offered to redouble his efforts to

find out any information about Handsome and to come back and tell us.

'Best not,' said Grandma. 'Just keep in touch with Malcolm and let him know of any developments.'

'Good thinking, Grandma,' I said. 'One crooked friend of the family is probably enough for Mum to cope with. No offence, Mr Eassle.'

'William Walter Eassle,' he smiled happily. 'But call me Willie. All my friends do.' And he went off jauntily, to rid himself of the smell of cat's-pee perfume, and to ditch Marlene.

29

Just a week to go now till Christmas. Cosgrove High is buzzing. The hall is piled up with Christmas boxes for the pensioners. Mum had insisted on putting hankies in with my stick-on snake tattoos. Some people had wrapped their presents up in shoe boxes, and the image of the shoe box Mum had given me floated across my mind. But I pushed it away. I'd open that box soon, but not now.

The walls of the hall are covered in cheerful paper Santas. Velvet and I made ours together in Art. Velvet did the drawing, she's good at that, and I helped paint it and stick on the cotton-wool beard.

I wanted to do something different, like give our Santa an eye patch and a black moustache, but Velvet said that wouldn't look right. She said that Santas should be traditional, so I gave him a large ring with a skull and crossbones on it instead. I'd seen a Santa in the town centre once with a ring like that. Belinda's Santa had 'In the Pink' written on all the presents spilling out of his sack, till Mad Max made her paint it out. I like Mad Max. He's scruffy like me.

'We are decorating the school hall for Christmas,' he told Belinda. 'Not advertising your mum's shop.'

Quite right too. But I still have to go in there. I have the money for Mum's beauty voucher now, but I still haven't bought it, though Velvet's offered to go with me.

'For protection,' she giggled. 'Just in case something pink jumps out and threatens to beautify you.'

The teachers could do with being beautified. They're tearing their hair out because no one wants to do any work. Mrs Jackson tried to get us to write an essay on 'What we'd like for Christmas'. That was a disaster.

'I'd hoped to get some mention of freedom from poverty, hunger, oppression, or perhaps a mention of world peace, but all I got was everybody's Christmas list,' she said sadly.

What did she expect? She was lucky anyone actually did the homework. What with practising for the Christmas concert, decorating the school hall and getting ready for the disco, who has time for school work? Really, teachers can be so unrealistic sometimes. Don't they know there are only twenty-four hours in every day? Except Saturdays, which I'm sure only have twenty hours – see Abigail Montgomery's *Theory of Time*!

Miss Flack came round with my outfit for the Christmas disco last night. I'd chosen the material for the trousers myself; a deep burgundy velvet.

'Beautiful,' said Miss Flack. 'Very Christmassy. Jewel colours are just right at this time of year.'

'But I didn't see anything I liked for the top,' I'd wailed. 'What will I do?'

'Would you trust me to buy something?' Miss Flack had asked.

I nodded. She had some brilliant ideas.

But not this time!

When she opened up the parcel and took out the blouse she'd made for me, it was pink. Pink and frilly!

The expression on my face must have said it all. Even Mum and Grandma kept quiet.

'Try it on before you decide.' Miss Flack was soothing. 'If you hate it I have time to make you something else.'

I took the outfit upstairs and tried it on. Trousers first. They were great. They fitted like a dream. Miss Flack had put a little zip on a side pocket. The zip had a little trail of pink beads hanging from it. Hmm, nice. Then I looked at the blouse. Pink and frilly. Yuck! I couldn't possibly wear it. I closed my eyes and put it on. Then I peeked in the mirror. WOW!! The blouse was very fitted and clung like a second skin. The sleeves had little zips in them with a trail of burgundy beads, and the deep frill made my bosom look as good, if not better than, Belinda Fishcake's.

I shot back downstairs and hugged Miss Flack.

'It's fantastic,' I said. 'I look fantastic. You're fantastic, Miss Flack.'

'Fantastic Miss Flack,' squawked Mortimer.

And Miss Flack blushed as we all joined in the chorus of 'Fantastic Miss Flack'.

30

I love Christmas. I love putting up the tree and hunting for the box of Christmas decorations up in the loft. The loft is full of junk; my old doll, my old doll's pram and my real pram as well. Grandma's old trunk is up there too. We didn't know in the beginning if Grandma was staying with us for good, but it just sort of happened that she did, and her old trunk was bumped up into the loft. She goes up there sometimes to have a look through it when she's really missing Handsome Harris. There's still no word of him. Grandma contacted a few friends in Oz, and they made some enquiries, but so far, nothing. And I know that Mum, unbeknown to Grandma, has been making enquiries too, with no success. But Grandma refuses to be downhearted.

'Handsome is indestructable,' she says. 'He'll be right.' And she keeps herself busy just like Ms Tickle told her.

She was doing her best to be cheerful for Christmas. She had untangled the fairy lights and got them working, then she and I sat down with the box of Christmas decorations and sifted through them.

'I made this in Year 1,' I said, holding up a piece of egg box covered in tin foil. 'It's supposed to be a Christmas bell.'

'It's lovely,' said Grandma. 'Weren't you clever. Hang it on the tree.'

'And here's the little knitted stockings Mum made. She always fills them with sweets.'

'And I thought you believed Santa's elves did that,' laughed Mum, bringing in some new tinsel she'd bought.

'I did till I noticed the elves liked the same sweets as you.'

'Give us a sweet. Give us a sweet,' squawked Mortimer.

The three of us dressed the tree and stood back to admire it.

'Well,' said Mum. 'It might not be the most elegant tree in the street, but it's definitely the nicest.'

'Even if the fairy does look like she's been at the sherry,' grinned Grandma.

'Give us a sherry. Give us a sherry,' squawked Mortimer.

'That's not a bad idea,' said Mum, and she and Grandma had a glass each. I had a Coke. Sherry smells disgusting.

But it made Mum and Grandma quite chatty.

'Are you looking forward to Christmas Eve and David and his family coming round?' asked Grandma.

'Oh yes,' said Mum. 'Especially as you're doing the cooking.'

'We've never had a Christmas barbie before,' I said. 'It'll be fun. Not that it wasn't before,' I added hastily, in case I hurt Mum's feelings.

'What are you giving David for Christmas?' asked Grandma.

'I'm not saying,' said Mum. 'It's not quite ready yet.'

'You haven't been to carpentry classes again,' I said.

Years ago Mum had made me a doll's house for Christmas. But, when I put the furniture in, the walls collapsed and the roof fell in.

'No,' said Mum. 'I don't really think carpentry's quite my thing. This is something else.'

Curiouser and curiouser. She'd been disappearing up to her room a lot recently, but I thought she was working at her law books. I wonder what she was really up to.

I'd bought Andy a shower radio in the shape of a penguin. I hoped he'd like it. I don't know what he's bought me, but I know it's got something to do with stones. He was being very mysterious about it last Saturday, but that's the only clue he would give me. Stones. Hmm. Maybe it's a bit of fossilized dinosaur bone. He likes that kind of thing. Or, maybe he's made something with pebbles from the beach. Or, maybe it's one of those little stone animals like a whale or a rhino. Or, maybe . . . maybe I'd just better wait and see. Not long to go now.

The school Christmas disco was great. Some people

came wearing headbands with Rudolph antlers on them. I, of course, was too elegant to indulge in that. Andy loved my trousers and shirt.

'You'll be the prettiest one there,' he said when he picked me up.

He says the nicest things sometimes.

Belinda and the Beelines were there in matching glittery frocks and shoes.

Belinda eyed up my outfit. 'Another designer model, I suppose,' she sneered. 'Where did you get that pink top from?'

'Wouldn't you like to know,' I said, and walked on with Andy.

See, unperturbed. Like I said.

But we had a great time at the disco and danced till we dropped. There's something about the Christmas disco with everyone singing 'So here it is, Merry Christmas, everybody's having fun', that makes it really special.

On the way home in the taxi Andy gave me my present. It's in a tiny box wrapped in gold paper with a Santa sticker on the front. There's a little label on it that says, 'To Abby, love Andy xx'.

'But don't open it till Christmas morning,' said Andy.

'Don't you open yours either,' I said to him later, when I gave him his shower radio. He'd come in to our house for a Coke and a mince pie before he went home, and to wish Mum and Grandma a happy Christmas.

Then I gave him a clue about his present. I said it had to do with water. I think he thinks it's new swimming goggles.

Then, standing in the hall, we said goodnight. It took us ages. Neither of us wanted to leave the other. I had this really excited, tingly feeling inside. So did Andy. But eventually he had to go. Mum drove him home. I just love Christmas and everything about it. Did I mention that before?

31

It's Christmas Eve. I'm on holiday from school and there's so much to do. First I have to meet Velvet in town to go and buy Mum's beauty voucher. I'd put it off till the last minute. I went into town on the bus and met Velvet outside the music shop, in the High Street. She was wearing a long, warm coat and a stripy woollen hat, pulled down low, over her ears. Sensible girl. My ear lobes were numb with the cold.

Velvet and I clowned about outside 'In the Pink' and she pretended to drag me inside. It was really busy with women getting beautified for Christmas. Some of them were having false nails glued on. I hoped the glue was strong. Imagine coming across one of those in your Christmas dinner. Turkey with chestnut and nail stuffing. Yuck! Some were having their toenails painted bright blue. Aren't feet ugly. Mine are long and thin like the rest of me. It's as well they're covered up most of the time.

Other ladies were having facials. They were relaxing in reclining chairs, pink gowns covering their clothes and pink towels protecting their hair while beauticians smeared their faces in goo. One woman was bright turquoise. I hoped her face wouldn't stay that colour.

Belinda was behind the desk, looking important.

'Can I help you?' she asked. She was wearing a bright pink tunic with 'In the Pink' embroidered in deeper pink spidery writing on the pocket. 'If you've come for a total makeover in time for Christmas, I'm afraid we can't help you. We don't do miracles.'

'Unperturbed, remember,' whispered Velvet in my ear.

'I want a gift voucher for my mum,' I said, through gritted teeth.

'Oh,' she said. 'A gift voucher. I don't do gift vouchers. I'll get one of our junior assistants to help you.'

Junior assistants! Just who did she think she was? Any more junior than than she was and they'd still be in the womb!

I watched as she bounced over on her platform trainers to a girl who was folding pink towels. She came over to us and organized the gift voucher.

'Well, what do you think of that?' I exploded, when Velvet and I got outside. 'Little Miss Perfect, acting like she ran the place. Little Miss High and Mighty. Little Miss—'

Velvet nudged me in mid-rant and pointed at the window. Inside we could see Belinda's mum giving her a brush and telling her to sweep up the floor. We stood and watched till we knew she had seen us. She pretended she hadn't. But she had, and we knew she had, and she knew we knew she had, if you see what I mean.

I took Velvet's arm. 'Come on,' I said. 'We're all finished here. Time to get Grandma's present.'

I'd thought long and hard about what to get for Grandma. She wasn't the smelly perfume/soap/bubble-bath type, so I bought her a teddy. I know you'll think she was far too old for a teddy, but I thought, if you're feeling a bit low, as Grandma was, you can always give a teddy a cuddle. You're never too old for a cuddle. Anyway there was one I really fancied – for Grandma, that is. He was a fluffy caramel colour and had a cute kind of 'I need a cuddle' expression. All right, so that might just have been my over-fertile imagination, but I bought him anyway.

Then Velvet and I exchanged gifts, wished each other a happy holiday, and went off home. It was almost dark when I reached our house. It looked lovely with the Christmas tree in the window, and some old fairy lights illuminating the laurel bush by the front door. Grandma had also lit up the Pets' Problems sign so it flashed off and on in tiny white lights. The air was crisp and cold. Not cold enough for snow, the weather man said, but dry. A good night for a barbecue.

When I went indoors everyone was busy. Mum was stacking up crockery and cutlery in the kitchen ready for the barbie. Grandma was preparing steaks, sausages, kebabs, and enough rolls to feed an army. I said a quick hullo and bounded upstairs to wrap up my presents. Then I came down and placed them under the tree. By that time, Mum was in a panic; the guests would be here soon, and she wasn't properly dressed yet. She told me to hunt out napkins and glasses and she hurried upstairs. Ten minutes later she was back, poured into a short black sequined dress with a plunging neckline. And not a lot else.

'You can't go outside for a barbie in that,' I protested. 'You'll freeze. I'll go and get you a big woolly cardigan to put on over it.'

'No, you won't,' grinned Grandma. 'Leave your mum alone, Abby. She looks lovely.'

Mum smiled at Grandma, and, for a moment, she didn't look like my mum at all. She looked like . . . I don't know, she looked different . . . like a modern-day Cinderella in spiky heels. Then the doorbell rang, and her prince arrived. Not in a golden coach, but in a beat-up old Range Rover, splattered in mud. Prof Charlie and Peter were there too. They came in carrying pressies and chocolates and wine. If you used your imagination, the Prof, with his white hair and bag of pressies, could be mistaken for Santa Claus.

'We'll open the presents at midnight,' said Grandma. 'Meantime, let's get cooking.'

Grandma had made Mum a nut roast, but the rest of us had the sausages, steaks and kebabs.

Grandma and Charlie cooked. Mum and David organized the music and poured the wine.

Mum shivered, as I told her she would, in the cold night air, but David took off his old leather jacket, put it round her shoulders, and hugged her close. Now, wasn't that romantic? I wonder if Mum planned that. Maybe she did know a thing or two after all. Hmm.

Then we had hot Christmas pud with cold ice-cream on the side. Lovely. After that we played Twister till we all fell over, exhausted.

Before we knew it, it was midnight, and everyone hugged and kissed each other – some took longer than others, soppy things – and wished each other a happy Christmas. I started opening my pressies. Andy's first because I was really curious. What *was* inside that box, and what did it have to do with stones? I opened up the box and a little heart-shaped locket with a red stone in the middle winked at me. Inside the locket was a cut-out photo of Andy and me that had been taken ages ago. Now, wasn't that romantic? I blushed and hoped that no one had noticed.

David opened up the present Mum had given him. It was a fancy knitted sweater in blue, to match his eyes! So that's what she'd been working on all this time. David put it on immediately, and said it was lovely. It wasn't. It was horrible. Love really is blind after all.

Then Grandma opened up the teddy, and was reading the label I'd written and tied round his neck – 'To keep you company till Handsome gets here' – when the doorbell rang.

'Who on earth is that at this time of night?' said Mum. 'Perhaps it's the neighbours. Perhaps we're making too much noise.'

140

'I'll get it,' I said, and went to open the door before Mum could protest.

A tall, weatherbeaten man stood there, clutching some parcels. He had a nose that had obviously been broken in several places, an ear with a bit missing, and a lopsided smile.

'Hi,' he said. 'I'm sorry to call so late, but your light was on. You must be Abby. Is your grandma home? I'm Handsome Harris.'

Whaaaaat? Rearrange these words into a well-known phrase or saying:

Feather with me knocked down you could have a.

I stood with my mouth open like Danny Plover in 3B.

When I'd recovered my senses I yelled, 'GRANDMA!'

Grandma came running, then Mum, then Benson, then everybody else. Mortimer squawked, 'What's up, what's up!'

Everyone opened their mouth in amazement when they saw Handsome Harris. Everyone, that is, except Grandma. She just screamed with delight and hurled herself at him. He picked her up in the biggest bear hug in the history of the universe. Then he kissed her. A great smacking 'it's wonderful to see you' kind of kiss. It was just so romantic. I didn't know old people did romantic. But they do. I was quite tearful. It was all so . . . nice. Then everyone was laughing and talking at the same time.

Over a cold beer and a warm mince pie, Handsome

told us he'd stopped writing because he thought he might have been overlooked addressing a letter to Grandma one day, and he didn't want any crooks turning up here. I immediately thought of Malcolm and Willie the Weasel.

Grandma obviously did too, but she winked at me and said nothing. Then Handsome'd got a job on a construction site in the middle of nowhere, and saved up enough money to fly over.

'I thought I'd surprise you, Aphrodite,' he grinned.

'You certainly did,' laughed Grandma. 'But you're the best Christmas present I could have had.'

Great. She wouldn't be needing the teddy then! I'd taken a real fancy to him.

The party went on until the wee small hours. There's something magical about Christmas. Something indefinable in the air. I stood at the back door and looked out at the night sky. It was cold and clear and the stars looked very close. I wished I knew all their names. The smell of the barbie hung in the air, mingled with the Christmas smells of scented candles and warm mince pies. I listened to the laughter and the chatter coming from the sitting room and I thought about how things change. How different this year was to last, when Mum and I were on our own. Now we were surrounded by family and friends and pets.

It *was* magical. It was the very best thing about Christmas.